The Professionals

Grace Cha

ISBN: 0692252584
ISBN 13: 9780692252581
Library of Congress Control Number: 2014912528
Grace Cha, Concord, CA

1

There was a time in Helena Park's life when she was completely content being silent. Not having to overreact or show off or start a conversation to fill in awkward silences. She usually left that to other people, one of her more charismatic friends, and, those who were so uncomfortable with peace and quiet that they felt they had to pipe in every few moments just to see if anyone on the receiving end was home. There was a time in Helena's life when she believed in her ability to create something through what most people would deem as artistic expression, whether it was drawing a portrait of Lou Reed off an album cover or writing poetry at intervals that just spilled out of her when writing journal entries, which she had kept starting at age 12. She found the journal a healthy respite from her depression and hopelessness that had set in rather early on in her life. She had withstood her latch key childhood and her parents' unhealthy inherent narcissism and preoccupation with their own relationship, believing it was neglect. .

When she met Tom Overton, it was no accident. They were brought together in a situation where Helena knew of her circumstances quite well. There was no party, no squalid need for a drunken encounter coated as one misguided night of romance, no guilty parties the next morning with sloppy morning whispers in her ear, no waiting to use a messy bathroom while she surveyed the equally putrid living quarters around her, scattered with cigarettes stubbed out messily in ashtrays, beer and liquor bottles, clothes strewn on the floor in a sordid array of carelessness. Those were days long gone, a time when she found herself running in those circles. She remembered as a teenager walking around her suburban neighborhood with two good friends smoking pot and sitting near the Mormon church around the corner from her house, the irony lost on them as they laughed, their voices cutting into the quiet, cold night violently like birds singing at a funeral. They had looked up at the dark twilight sky, black as ink, dotted with white stars, marveling at its expansiveness. The nights of her youth at that time were so still it scared her. She was afraid to disturb it, yet she wanted to scream and yell at the shrill complacence. There is a sound to silence, she remembered noting, just like there is a sound to sex, when both partners become reticent, too engaged in their actions to acknowledge just how possessed they are.

Those were days long gone, and every year that passed, she grew more and more distant from her days shrouded in youthful idealism, foolish dreams and the idea that she might become something "big." Still, she drifted in and out of reality, never quite disconnecting from the time of her careless youth.

∾

The large one-story house seemed flat, planted squarely in the middle of neatly trimmed pools of grass. Her house was the only one on the block within miles that had real grass. Shortly after moving in to this tract home, her father had stared out at the front yard, standing staunchly on the front porch. The lawn was nothing but brown dirt waiting to be dressed and adorned into greenery, so bare, it begged for landscaped foliage to brighten its sad forlorn mood. And so, her father made the decision to plant real grass seedlings because he wanted his lawn to be real. As the grass began to grow, Helena had noted its patchy, shorn, uneven appearance, and looked to the neighbors' lawns, their grass so neat and full and green like slightly overgrown putting greens. The other houses had that fake grass, the kind they rolled out onto those bare dirt floors. A concrete walkway curved its way to the front porch and front door. Plots filled with dirt and bushes were placed on either side. Large granite-like rocks floated among the bushes.

Inside, Korean artifacts peppered the home – polished wooden chests with old-fashioned brass locks, stuffed silk ornately embroidered butterflies with long strands of silk string hung on the walls. The living room was furnished with black polished lacquered furniture with designs cut from shell and jade and coral. Scroll paintings of a face of a tiger, fierce and determined, descending down a mountain with his strong body in tow. Red chiseled coral vases. Wooden statuettes of a traditional Korean man and woman. Large stuffed traditional dolls wearing costumes. Their hair, black slick thread shaped closely to their styrofoam heads, large painted eyes, tiny sweetheart red lips, staring out into the distance looking peaceful and content.

Her parents were travelers, and they brought home all kinds of souvenirs from all over the world. Her mother was an avid collector. The house was littered with collectors spoons from Europe, England, Russia, Asia. Wedgewood, shot glasses, mugs, candy tins bearing the faces of Prince Charles and Princess Diane. Shelves and display cases featured all kinds of little knick knacks from afar.

Judith Park often accompanied her husband, Mike, on his conferences abroad. Pictures of their travels hung on the walls, in front of the fountains in Italy, on the mountain tops in Korea, wind blowing their clothes and hair about, in front of rose gardens in England, standing in the snow in Russia bundled up so thickly with coats, a hat and scarf, they looked almost unrecognizable.

They were always having parties, Helena remembered. And traveling, leaving her with sitters. But on their return, they brought back an abundance of gifts, clothes, toys, souvenirs. It became a routine – her father, a professor of economics, went to conferences and her mother went along with him, and she would await their return and anticipate the gifts. That's what her young mind sped to, the gifts. She remembered a porcelain blue and white windmill from Holland that made music when the windmill was turned. Her little cousin, a terror at age five, had grabbed it and smashed it into the floor, breaking it into pieces.

Her parents had tried their best to give Helena everything they thought she should have. When they moved to that larger home in the northwest suburbs, in a more upscale neighborhood, they had a pool built in the backyard, a new puppy, and she had learned to ride her bike. She used to roller skate in the alleyway in the backyard on the side of the house. It was only a short distance, but she enjoyed strapping on her skates as soon as she got home from school to go that short distance, back and forth, until she got bored with it and flung off the skates, running inside to occupy herself with other things. She sometimes skated around the pool, though she knew it was dangerous. She got excited at the prospect of danger, skimming the corners of its sensible rectangular shape, getting as close to the edge as possible, her heart racing as she went around the deep end. She imagined herself slipping and falling into the cool water and sinking quickly as the heavy steel connecting the wheels to her feet dragged her down to the bottom. Would she be able to bend down in the water and untie the laces in time to release them and swim up to the surface? Or would she struggle and flail, submitting to the heavy pull downward, panicking, as she slowly drowned?

When she was 13, her parents had taken her on summer vacation to the Grand Canyon in Arizona. Mike Park had made it a point to visit the Native American reservations in the area. Helena had never seen such disparate poverty. Old men, women and children sat outside tin shacks; cloths and blankets covered open windows. Helena had stared at the faces, withered like worn brown leather, their eyes sullen and empty with exhaustion. They had stopped and bought some pottery from one of the women, but when her mother tried to take a picture, the woman became angry. Mike Park had told her later: "They don't want to be seen as spectacles, they're human, they're just living their lives. Why should we want to document them like they're some kind of zoo animal?"

They had driven away in silence, still with a kind of respect or sadness, Helena wasn't quite sure which. She would always remember that trip. The pottery they had purchased sat on a glass table in the living room that would always remind her.

They had also visited the petrified wood forest. She would marvel at the swirled yellow and blue colors of the petrified wood she had collected that she placed on a shelf in her bedroom. Their family vacations had always amused her. They had taken another trip to Vancouver for the World Expo, and it was somehow comical planning the trip and then sitting innocently in the back of the car as her father insisted on driving these long distances instead of flying. The hours dragged on as she stared at the back of her parents' heads. Those vacations were supposed to be fun, but they always turned out to be somehow educational, and somehow, like work.

∾

Helena ducked under the awning and closed her umbrella, shaking off the rain before stepping into the revolving door that led to her office.

As senior supervising consultant, a title she recently got promoted to just within the last few months, she was enjoying her time being a higher-up, with all its privileges – long lunches with the other managers, the weekends out of town, the clean and fresh hotel rooms she got to have special treatment in. Most of all, she loved training others, those just hired in the company, those that could contribute in meaningful ways, making the company better and more competitive.

Ever since the promotion, she decided it best to get more serious in life, and not wither away being stuck in a cubicle taking orders from others and playing office politics. She still had to deal with those kinds of things, but she had a clearer idea of who she was now, and others relied on her, were even dependent on her, to get the job done and to do it well.

She arrived at her desk and plunked down her briefcase. She wiped her dark hair back with both her hands and straightened her suit jacket, which hung well on her lithe figure. Then she checked her messages.

All of them were about matters already taken care of, just a follow up or two needed to be done – except for one.

They were looking to hire a new junior consultant in their satellite office in Chicago. The message was from her manager who told her she needed to fly out immediately and take care of hiring. They were already in the process of taking applications, but the interview and hiring process were to be her sole responsibility.

She sat down and bit her lip. She was to fly out by tomorrow. She was excited to see applicants, but she had just returned from Chicago and wanted some time to rest. So much for that. She prepared herself mentally and motivated herself with a reward upon her return to Los Angeles, a trip to a day spa.

She picked up the phone and asked her secretary Anastasia to book the flight.

2

~

Helena boarded the plane headed for Chicago. She had a copy of Newsweek and opted not to watch the movie. Soon, she was nodding off to sleep. She was awoken by the stewardess for lunch. Turkey and Swiss with lettuce, tomato on French bread, and a fruit cup. For a beverage, she chose cranberry juice.

The flight was pleasant and Helena was enjoying the time to herself before the hustle bustle of the city caught up with her.

When she disembarked, she suddenly felt awkward and self-conscious. She had to admit she sometimes got nervous when meeting with the other managers and all the employees at the office. She was a petite woman, and sometimes felt the men's stature and height intimidating. There were certain people she liked better than others, and some that she had little tolerance for. One that she had little tolerance for was Kip, one of the managers in the Chicago area. He was always looking her up and down, not in a sexual way per se, but in a judgmental way. He looked at her in a way that asked, who put you in charge? Or, what do you know?

When she arrived at her hotel room, she called in to Gerard Ripling, another manager.

"You made it!" he said, jovial.

"Well, yes."

They would start interviewing applicants tomorrow at 9 a.m. It was going to be a long day. He asked her how the flight was, the weather in L.A., others at corporate. Long, unusually gloomy, and good, were her answers. They said see you tomorrow and hung up.

Helena had a hard time sleeping. She had struggled with mild insomnia as a teenager, and was at one time diagnosed with severe depression. Sometimes, it came back to haunt her. Her remedy now was to take an over the counter antihistamine when it became unbearable. She eventually took one at midnight, and dropped off to sleep.

It wasn't until her college years that she began taking medication after a nervous breakdown. She held herself up fine over the years, except the insomnia that seemed to plague her despite it all. She found satisfaction in work and, against doctor's orders, continued to pursue a career competitively despite her condition. Her "condition" was exacerbated particularly when one was under high stress. This "condition" as Helena referred to it, could be managed by medication and she had no intention of leaving her job or settling for a less stressful and potentially less prestigious one because of it. But if she was not careful, she could all but do herself in.

She arrived at the office at a quarter to nine. Gerard was there and greeted her warmly. There was a maze of cubicles and chattering voices, ringing phones and clacking of computer keyboard keys. She straightened her posture and relaxed.

"How goes everything?" she asked Gerard.

"Pretty good. Except for this turnover," he said. "I mean, we go through all this training and then it's a waste. They're gone the next day."

"I know," Helena shook her head knowingly. "Well, maybe this next one will be a good one. One we can hang on to."

"Let's hope."

Some other managers and assistants began milling around as 9 o'clock approached. Soon after, they entered a conference room and took their seats.

The first interview was scheduled for 9:30. The first half hour was for a managers' meeting. Gerard stood up and went over the Chicago operations – numbers, momentum, instructions from corporate and so on. He acknowledged Helena, who would be the deciding vote for the final selection of the new associate for their office.

As 9:30 approached, the other managers trickled out of the conference room and Gerard, Kip and Helena were left alone. They took sips of water and waited patiently. A secretary soon approached at about 9:25 and said someone was waiting in the lobby. The first interviewee.

A tall young man with golden hair strolled into the room. He was holding a briefcase and she noticed his eyes. He was wearing a yellow tie with blue print and a light blue oxford shirt. Beige slacks. Polished black shoes.

He offered his hand to Gerard.

"Good morning," he said.

Gerard took his hand in a firm grip, and then the young man turned to Kip, shook his hand, and then finally to Helena and shook her hand. He looked straight into Helena's eyes.

He had the face of a cupid. His eyes burst from his skull like sharp, blue meteor bombs. They were wide and you could tell that if you stared long enough, you would fall in deep, like a well that went to the core of the earth.

"Have a seat," she said.

Then the interview began.

His name was Thomas Overton – Tom, he corrected. He was a graduate of the University of Connecticut, then moved to Chicago. Business major. Then went on to law school.

"Tell us about your experience," said Kip.

"I just left a job doing inside sales for a television channel," he answered. "But before that, I worked at Shane & Wilkinson as a junior consultant."

"How long were you there for?" Gerard asked.

"Shane & Wilkinson - four years. KROE – two."

They grilled him about the basics, what did he know about the business, how many contracts had he closed successfully, about the company, what did he think he could contribute.

Then Helena explained how the job would work. Tom shifted in his seat and stared at her. She quickly finished, almost running out of breath, and then asked if he had any questions.

"How many branches do you have?"

"Three – L.A., Chicago and New York."

"And are you all based here?"

"Helena is from our L.A. branch," said Kip, pointing in her direction.

"Oh."

"Well!" said Gerard. "You were our first interview of the day, so we still have some other applicants to interview. We're very glad to have met you, Tom. And we'll be in touch."

"Thank you...very much, I appreciate your time," he said, standing up and shaking everyone's hand again.

"Goodbye."

"What do you think?" Kip asked, taking a sip of water.

"He has experience," said Gerard. "Seemed like a nice guy."

Helena was quiet.

"Well, we still have more to interview," she said.

"Right."

The day progressed with a total of 10 applicants. They breezed in and out the entire day, men and women, short and tall, old and young. By the time the last one was out the door, it was 5:30 p.m.; they were all dizzy.

Helena was beat. Gerard and Kip invited her to dinner, but she said she would get room service. She was to meet them tomorrow to discuss who they wanted to hire. Again, at 9 a.m.

Back at the hotel room Helena took a hot shower and ordered a salad. After her shower, she walked out to her balcony in her bathrobe when she heard knocking on the door. She went to answer it and met with the room service attendant for her dinner. She sat down at the table and dug into her salad. After dinner, she turned on the news. Her thoughts turned to the events of the day. Kip and Gerard would be asking who she wanted to hire. She couldn't stop thinking about Tom Overton.

She remembered her friend, Chaz, telling her that when she met the right person, she would "know." There was no rhyme or reason to it, it was fate, and destiny and God's plan all working together that would let her know that that person was "the one."

This must be it, she thought. Tom Overton was "the one." Then she began to retread. This is ridiculous, she thought. She hardly knew him. But things like that didn't matter, Chaz had implied. It's all happenstance. When that spark hits, then the ball is in the air and all it takes is for her or him to catch it and throw it. Soon, they would be throwing evenly and that's the way you answer to destiny. Destiny doesn't happen by sitting and letting things happen, it happens only with the aid of one's works. If you felt something, and just sat on it, doing nothing, then it slips past you and nothing ever happens in your life. You get buried by the lost opportunities and, as in Helena's case, you remain unhappy, alone.

This had happened to Helena before. She had a penchant for self-sabotage. She didn't believe she deserved good things, or to be happy. She only found solace in work. She needed to learn how to make things happen in her personal life, her love life, her friend had told her.

Her cousin had told her once that she should only make friends with people who were better than her so that she could learn from them and become a better person and "move up" in the world, so to speak. She didn't take that advice. She still had friends who were working "blue collar" jobs. She hated sounding like a snob.

But she felt a sense of urgency. She was to be 35 in June. Something was telling her that she couldn't just "sit" on this one. She had to do something. She sat with this feeling of desperation until she fell asleep.

Helena's hand reached out for the phone, her wake-up call, at 7:45 a.m. Breakfast was on a tray outside her door. She ate quickly and got dressed. She climbed into her rental car and sped off to the office.

There were donuts and coffee in the conference room. Helena took a seat and took out copies of the resumes that they had accumulated the day before. Kip and Gerard walked in and out of the room. They had matters to attend to. Helena paid no mind and acted as though she were studying the resumes. Finally, Kip and Gerard came in the room and closed the door. They sat down and each took what seemed like their fourth or fifth donuts. They pulled out their copies of the resumes.

"Whoever wants to start…" said Gerard.

"I liked this guy, Mason Andrews, he seemed really enthusiastic," said Kip.

"What did you think of him, Helena?" asked Gerard.

"Ehh," she motioned so-so with her hand. "He's going to have a long commute," she added.

"True," said Gerard.

What they didn't know, was that Helena had come up with an excuse *not* to hire every applicant except for Tom Overton. She had gone over her notes carefully and had even made some up on her notepad during the interviews.

When they came to Tom Overton's resume, Helena said she thought he was very bright and had potential to move up in the company with his educational background.

"You can't really beat a law degree," she said, peering over her horn-rimmed eyeglasses.

"A business major, then law, then television? He doesn't seem like he knows where he's going," said Kip.

"Precisely why we should hire him. Give him a chance to grow here. He's someone who can be nurtured. He's open to learning, he even said so himself," Helena said. "I really like him. I think he would get along with others, and he's adaptable, considering the varied experience he's had." She threw his resume on the table resolutely.

There was a pause.

Kip took a sip of coffee. Gerard scratched his chin.

"Well, you're it. It's your call. We'll hire him."

"Great," Helena said. "I want him in training by Friday, and I'll be there, too. Along with Allen."

They all agreed that Gerard would make the call.

∞

Tom Overton's cell phone rang on Wednesday afternoon.

He was having lunch alone at a diner downtown.

"Hello."

"Tom Overton?"

"Yes this is he."

"This is Gerard from Advent Solutions."

"Hello, how are you?"

"Great. Listen, we've made a decision, and we would like to hire you if you're still interested in working with us."

"Yes, I am."

"OK, then, welcome aboard! We'll have a training session that will begin on Friday at 9 a.m. in the same place we interviewed you at. Do you remember where that was?"

"I do. Yes."

"OK. We'll see you then."

"Sure. See you then."

Tom Overton tapped his smartphone screen to hang up. He looked down at his burger and fries and suddenly was not hungry anymore. He was slightly nervous about starting a new job. This company really seemed to have it together. Mostly, though, he was surprised to have been picked out of what seemed like a large pool of applicants. He suddenly wasn't sure he could pull it off. He tried to remember his experience at Shane & Wilkinson, how much he hated it at first, and then the swift satisfaction he felt after closing a contract.

The waitress came by and asked if he wanted to wrap up his food to go. He said no, then reached in his pocket for his wallet and paid the bill. He picked up his messenger bag, and left.

By the time he arrived at his apartment it was dusk. He had studied the company Web site and had a pretty good idea of what the company was about. That one lady, his higher up, Helen-something, she had explained it pretty well. He dropped his briefcase on the bedroom floor of his one-bedroom apartment. It was sparsely furnished and the most intrusive item was a large flat screen TV and a DVD collection spanning the length of the wall. He had a smaller shelf that held a hand-ful of books. Above his bed hung an American flag and some concert posters.

He sat and sifted through his mail. He won-dered what he should have for dinner. He had been eating this frozen gnocchi from the health food store for weeks now, and decided he would eat that, again. If he remembered correctly, there was one last package in the freezer.

After dinner, his mind wandered to that lady at the job interview. He found her attractive, and felt a little uncomfortable during the interview. He guessed he wouldn't be seeing much of her since she was from the Los Angeles office. She seemed kind of intense, but reserved, as if she didn't know what she had unless someone told her or guided her toward it. She had been places, but she was living a better life, one that she had earned and she was very serious about retaining her status. He wondered what she was like in her off-hours, at a party or, drunk. He turned on the television to watch the late night news, and quickly forgot about her. She was in a different city. He left it at that.

∞

Helena was sitting at the front of the conference room with Gerard and Kip and Allen, a manager from the Chicago office. There were other new hires from L.A. and Chicago who joined them.

Tom Overton walked into the office at five minutes to nine and looked up at Helena. They locked eyes and then it was Helena who looked away.

"OK, we're going to get started pretty soon here," she announced. "You'll find folders on the table at your seats. Inside is a note pad, I suggest that you take notes."

They started out with a Power Point presentation and explained their expectations of their consultants. Then there was a question and answer session. Tom participated in earnest, asking for details because he wanted to give a good impression.

Helena felt an intense attraction to Tom. She felt as though bolts of electricity were shooting through her body. She excused herself and went to the bathroom. She leaned against the wall and took a couple of deep breaths. What would happen if she were to get together with him? Why was she falling for her employee? She remembered that this was her intention from the beginning.

She looked in the mirror and fixed her hair. She came out of the bathroom and returned to the conference room.

She was taken back to a time, only a couple of years ago, when she was working as a junior consultant herself. She was meeting with a client, he was an older man, but very attractive. They were talking and he was very polite. She was visiting his home and his family was there. He was married and had a teenage son and a ten-year-old daughter. He told her that they were getting ready to go to church. They invited her to go with them, but Helena thought it too informal considering their relationship. But she felt attracted to him, and wanted to call him and ask him to lunch or coffee alone, to talk. She didn't.

Then one day, he dropped in on her at work. Sam, a co-worker, had helped her with the account, and he had an idea of what was going on. He had the cubicle next to her and saw the man walk toward them.

"Uh-oh, here comes trouble," he joked, his pen hung from his mouth as he chewed on it. He leaned back in his chair, looked at her, and winked.

The man sat with Helena in her cubicle.

"I lost the paperwork you gave me last time we met," he said.

"I can get it for you," she had said.

He moved closer to her so that he was leaning over her shoulder. She felt his breath on her neck.

He reached out and pointed his index finger at the computer screen.

"Is this it?" he asked.

"Yes."

"Is there any way I can see it closer?" he asked.

She stopped what she was doing and froze. She paused.

"That's as close as it gets," she answered firmly. She printed out the report and gave him his copies.

"Can I call you if I want to change my plan?"

"Yes."

He smiled, folded the papers, put them in his coat pocket and left. When she had free time at work, she thought of him, wondering if he would call. He never did.

The warmth and electricity of that time was what she was feeling in the room right now with Tom.

Tom sat in his chair and remained calm. He felt her. He wished he knew what she was thinking – she put up a good front.

At break everyone stood up and went to the bathroom, got more coffee or picked at the sandwiches they had bought for lunch. Helena approached Tom and stood by his seat. She had her hands folded in front of her.

"So, how's it going?" she asked.

"Good."

"You starting to get a feel for what it's all about here?"

"Yeah, sure. It's sinking in."

"So, I've been meaning to ask you – how did a business and law major end up in television?"

"Well," Tom laughed. "That's a good question," he stopped and cleared his throat. "It just kind of ended up happening that way. I majored in business for my grandfather, law school for my parents and TV for myself."

"So I guess the question is, who's the most important to you now."

"I'd actually love to be a writer, but everyone wants to be a writer. If you're asking me if I'm committed to this job, 100 percent yes."

Helena smiled and nodded.

"I see you've dabbled in writing some from your resume."

"Yeah, that was just a small gig." He paused. They stared at each other awkwardly. "I'm looking forward to working here."

Helena paused.

"We're glad to have you," she said.

Soon break ended and training part two began. The session went smoothly and before they knew it, the training was over. Tom fought to remain focused on what he was learning but he was distracted by Helena.

As he put on his blazer and packed up his briefcase, Helena approached him again.

"We're looking to fly you out to L.A. next week. There'll be some new hires there, and we want you all to get some extended training. Is that going to be alright?"

"No problem."

"Great. Gerard and Kip will let you know."

On his way home, Tom couldn't stop thinking about her. He wondered if this "trip" to L.A. meant anything. Would she show up at his hotel room, wearing only a trench coat with nothing on underneath? Would she call him and invite him for drinks? Who was he kidding? This was strictly business. He couldn't help but think that maybe he had a chance. At the TV station, things like this happened all the time. Co-workers going out for drinks, getting together on the sly, clandestine relationships fed rumors, many of which turned out to be true. He, himself got involved with a production assistant, nothing serious, just a fling. At least he felt he was prepared for these kinds of office games. It could actually end up being quite amusing.

3

~

Elise Rudolph tapped away at her computer keyboard. She adjusted her headphone and mic. It was almost near the end of the day and she had three articles to send back to writers with their edits. She was growing tired (as she usually did at this time of the day) of making people sound literate and reinforcing what made a good article. More sources, better tone that flew with the story subject. Dig deeper. She didn't want to be a villain or a tyrant, but she had to be tough.

She had been working at the Sun Valley Herald for one year now and was beginning to feel some satisfaction from editing and assigning the local community stories that were the crux of the paper. Sometimes she felt it was her fault for not finding better stories, but truthfully, not a whole lot happened with the local beat in Sun Valley, except when elections rolled around. Every once in a while, sure, there was a man bites dog story, but rarely. After all, they were a community paper.

Years ago, she was talking to a friend, also a writer, where she happened to mention a "community" paper that another friend was working at, and that friend promptly quipped: "Nobody reads that."

Though the Sun Valley Herald was much larger than the one she had mentioned to that one friend, it was still small. But as an editor, she was still sharpening her teeth so to speak, so she told herself that this was her time to learn and grow. She actually liked the small staff, it was more intimate and she enjoyed her chance to hob nob with the community. And yes, people did read the paper, they had a loyal suburban audience.

She tapped and deleted, backspaced and entered. Finally! Done! One down, two to go. She sent it back to the writer and waited for the final draft. In the meantime, she would get an ice coffee. She pulled two dollars from her purse and made her way to the cafeteria.

When she returned to her desk, there was a message waiting for her. She picked up her phone and dialed her voicemail.

"Hi Elise, it's Blythe, just returning your call."

Elise punched in the phone Helena's number.

"Helena, it's Elise."

"Yeah, what's up? Any news?"

"Blythe just called me and left me a message. What do you want me to say to her?"

"Tell her you have a friend who knows a guy who is exceptional, and that you would like her to recruit him for a job at your paper, just like she did with you."

"I don't know if she'll do it."

"She did it with you."

"Yea, but I went to her. We don't usually use headhunters, especially for an entry-level position," Elise said.

"Tell her you just don't have time to do it, and you'll pay her."

"Well, I'll have to be sly about it. OK, I'll try and call her later today, if I get a chance, I'm pretty busy."

"Sure, take your time, and thank you."

"Yeah, yeah."

"Let me know what happens."

Elise took off her headset and leaned back in her chair. She had heard all about Helena's "situation," and agreed to "do what she could." Even though there was not an opening at the Herald – that was up to Elise to take care of. Make an opening, Helena had said. Who are we, the mafia? She had asked. You've got to do it, Helena had pleaded.

All this for a guy she barely knew.

As for making an opening, Elise had some ideas, but she had to be careful. This would take some days and nights of careful thought. Who was a good target? There were interns, but they were off-limits because Helena had made it clear that it had to be a paid position, and a reporter position. Helena had done her research. On a search of the

Internet, she had found some random restaurant and nightspot reviews in Chicago with the byline "Tom Overton." So he had some experience. How did she know that was him? Elise had asked her. How could it not have been? He lives in Chicago. Obviously while moonlighting in sales he was trying to grease the wheels of a writing career. It was so transparent how could she not see it? Helena had asked.

She could see the Herald without Fred in lifestyle, but he was one of the few who had been nice to her, that is, complacent, when she first arrived. What about Ray in business? Sometimes, he was too damn diligent. It would be a whole lot easier, she thought, if she targeted someone she disliked. There were a few that irritated her, but they were mostly the ones that had been there a while and they knew how to maneuver within the system too well.

Then the light bulb flicked on: the clerk. He was it. He would go. Not a reporter position, not an intern – just right in between.

Elise smiled to herself. Now she would have to come up with a plan.

∾

"You owe me," Elise told Helena over the phone later that night.

"I most definitely do. I hope this won't ruin you."

"We'll see what happens – it's not going to happen overnight."

"So what's your plan?"

"Oh, just some mild taunting. I'm going to assign him a story, clerks report stories every once in a while, and maybe engage in some e-mail harassment."

"Think you'll get caught? What if he complains?"

"Well, I'm in a higher position and luckily, I've also been there longer. He just got hired. Well, a year ago, but he's still sort of new."

"Green."

"I have to give him some credit though. He's not stupid. But I'll consider it a challenge."

"What do clerks do anyway?"

"They sort mail, answer phones, assist other reporters, mostly administrative stuff."

"Do they get promoted?"

"I don't see why they can't be. I mean, they're usually not satisfied with being clerks. Most want to move up and become reporters or copy editors. It depends on the person."

"I hope this gives Tom a chance."

"If he only knew what you're doing for him."

"It will all seem like things are falling in his lap," said Helena. "That's the way I want it."

"And then you'll pounce?"

"Once he's situated, *you* are the connection, 'Well what do you know my friend works there.' Get it?"

"Smooth." Elise paused. "Maybe you can actually help me oust him...his name's Chester...you know act like an angry source or a customer."

"Perfect! That would make it a lot easier on you."

They began devising a plan together. It was two hours later when the two finished their phone call. Elise would assign an article to Chester: a profile of Helena, or a "portrait of success," for the local beat. Helena would play phone tag with him until the very last minute of his deadline, causing him to flub the story. Elise would ask to look over it and change some vital information. Helena would call and complain, possibly even threaten to sue.

"What if he has an original draft that shows he got the information right?"

"You'll contend that it was wrong to begin with. I won't change anything. You will just have to stick to your side of the story while he will claim that what he wrote was accurate. It's not totally foolproof, but we can try it."

Helena insisted that it had to be foolproof. They decided to sleep on it and have further discussion the next day. She hung up and rubbed her eyebrows. She was feeling tense. She laid down and contemplated her plan. She smiled, and felt slightly smug.

∽

Tom Overton arrived at the airport just in time for lunch. He had breakfast on the plane, so he was not quite hungry yet. This was his first time visiting Los Angeles. He was excited and nervous at the same time. The weather was mild, a bit muggy, with a light breeze. Riding down the streets in his cab, he couldn't help but notice all the different types of people. A pudgy Hispanic woman pushed a stroller with kids in tow, waiting to cross the street. On the corner across from her, an artsy fellow with glasses wearing a camoflauge t-shirt and jeans pushed impatiently at the crosswalk button. As he walked across, Tom noticed a folded up magazine sticking out of his back pocket. An African-American gentleman wearing a suit and tie stood next to an old Asian lady carrying two plastic shopping bags in each hand at the bus stop. They all seemed to have one thing in common: they looked weary, like they had been stuck on some small planet for ages and were just waiting for confirmation that the spaceship had been fixed.

He asked the driver what part of the city they were in and he answered Hollywood. It was really the central part of the city, he added. He wondered where the beach was, and Beverly Hills. There was a lot to explore, he concluded.

"It's not usually this gloomy here," the cab driver said. "It's rare to have a day without sun."

They remained stuck in traffic for a good hour. When they finally made it to his hotel, Tom was relieved to be off the streets. It was chaotic and draining. There were amoebas of people swarming about, like an ant colony – organized chaos, but more chaotic than organized. But those were the people that didn't have access to a vehicle, for one reason or another, because he knew from friends that, no one prefers to walk in L.A. That's why they all looked so depressed, thought Tom. All the happy people were in their cars.

He wondered if he would have any time to go sightseeing. Maybe have time to visit a museum or go to the beach. Probably not.

When he arrived at his hotel room, there was a message waiting for him. It was from Helena. She told him to arrive at the office at 9 a.m. and gave him directions. She also added that he could get a cab to the office, but that someone could give him a ride back to the hotel after work. He was starting to get hungry and decided to go out and look for a place to eat. He changed into track shoes, jeans and a sweatshirt and headed out the door.

He looked ahead of him and saw a McDonald's hoping that wasn't the only place around to eat. He wished he had asked the cab driver if he could recommend any places he could go. He turned around and went back to the hotel.

"Excuse me," he asked the front desk clerk. "Do you know of any good places to eat around here, preferably one that serves beer?"

The desk clerk smiled. She told him about a place just around the corner. It was a Japanese-type of diner and they had some good teriyaki bowls and served alcohol. He thanked her and headed out.

The diner was full of young people, hipsters. All were absorbed in their conversations, rarely looking up. Tom smelled cooked meat and fried food. He sat at the sushi bar and ordered a beer, a spicy tuna roll and a California roll. As soon as he sat down, he became nervous, people started staring at him. Maybe wondering what his story was, alone, new to town. He looked at a blond girl seated next to him. She smiled.

"Hi," she said.

"Hey."

She turned back to a man seated next to her. She began talking animatedly.

"So, I had the audition, and the casting guy turns and says to me....you've got the look, but you don't have the chops...I was like, what?"

After a few sips of beer, his food finally arrived and Tom started to feel more comfortable. It was nice, being able to see another city through a job. He wondered if he would ever get tired of traveling like some of his friends. He had heard their stories about long flights, bad food, not knowing anything about the city, having to always eat in a hurry (usually fast food) and being unprepared for weather changes or transportation issues. Not to mention packing, the worst part of it, feeling like you were living out of a suitcase all the time. He could see how it could get old. But he wasn't there yet. He hated it when people always brought the down-side into a situation before you even got a chance to experience it. Call it critical thinking, or skepticism, people were always doing that just to show how smart they were in seeing something from different angles. Or maybe it was just a way to make conversation. At one time, he had thought that conversations were just private battles between people trying to show off. He often wished people would just keep their thoughts to themselves. Nonetheless, he had eventually graduated to the idea that conversation was essentially proof of who you were, and nobody wants to be just that, a nobody. He warmed up to this idea gradually, those who choose not to participate are basically doomed, whether they know it or not.

He took his time on the way home and enjoyed the evening breeze. He had a copy of the newspaper waiting for him back at the hotel and maybe he would make a cup of decaf. All in all, a decent day.

∾

"So what's the plan?" An anxious Helena was biting her nails. She had given up biting her nails years ago.

"Let's go with what we have," Elise said.

"Are you sure?"

"Yes. And the reason why I'm sure is because I already assigned him the article. You'll be getting a call tomorrow. But remember, screen it."

"I'm lucky I have Anastasia to take my calls."

There was a pause.

"You know, why didn't you just *not* hire the guy and then call him and ask him out?" asked Elise.

"Oh, no. I couldn't do that."

"Why not?"

"Could you?"

Elise paused for a moment. "Yeah, you're right. I'm too chicken."

"This is not just some *guy* Elise. This is him. The one. What chance do I have when he doesn't even live in the same city?"

"Okay, okay. Point made. It all just seems so radical."

"I can't sleep at night, I'm a mess over this guy."

"It's because you're crazy."

"What did I tell you about calling me that?"

"Sorry. So what are you doing this weekend?" Elise asked.

"Visiting my parents."

"Anniversary?"

"No, mom's birthday. Anyway, I haven't seen them in a long time."

"Have fun."

Yeah. See you soon, let's do lunch next week."

"Sure."

They both said good-bye and hung up.

4

~

The picture on Helena's mother's driver's license was one of bewildered pain. Her eyes were slightly red and glassy, as if in her head ran a circus of serious neurosis, so much so that it could be seen in those eyes, in the picture that identified her and justified her existence to the world, to the authorities, to any outsider who might have doubts as to her location in the map of her life. She wore a flowered dress as seen from the shoulders up, and her hair was a plain cut, a bob that shaped closely to her head. Her skin was red, but clear of any outstanding blemishes, as her mother was an obsessive skin care fanatic. She had beautiful skin, but in this picture the poor quality of the photograph, which made it grainy, showed a ruddy face, with a darker red revealing her prominent cheekbones, her mother's best feature.

Her wedding photos showed a stark contrast from the driver's license. Her skin was a soft, milky white, her eyes large and glowing, peaceful.

Picture after picture of every moment that takes place at a wedding were stored in a dusty album in the living room coffee table, aside from the ones framed and set on an end table in the family room. The bride before the ceremony, hair and make-up, the pictures on a stairwell of the wedding party, bridesmaids and flower girls, dressed in simple pepto-bismol pink dresses. Some men wore trendy black, thick glasses reminiscent of the 1950s. The ceremony, the walk down the aisle after the ceremony, the bride looking down, not daring to look up which would risk cursing the marriage with bad luck as an old tradition goes. There was one of the throwing of the bouquet from the stairwell to a group of eager women. Getting into the 1951 model blue Volkswagon Bug with white interior, ready to be driven off to the reception.

But there was the one photograph that Helena had always noticed the most. In a room, the photo almost appearing to have been taken at a fly on the wall angle, her mother stood against the door, apart from the crowd, while others milled around about her. Her husband greeted party goers and shook a man's hand, smiling. And her mother, at this time of social accompaniment, standing there with her head bowed down. How odd it looked! For at this time of happy congratulation, it seemed only appropriate that her mother as the bride join in the festivities, but she did not, was not, perhaps was simply instructed not to. She looked alone, lonesome, desolate. Had someone taken the photograph and with an x-acto knife cut away the party goers, isolating her in such a deposition, one would see something sad, something terribly wrong.

It was only twenty years later, when Helena could understand that bewildered pain that showed itself years later in the small square portrait that was her mother's driver's license picture.

Helena's father was a stoic proud man, to the point of being unable to crack his steely reserve. When Helena was nine years old, she had been afflicted with a bacteria in the form of worms in her intestinal tract. The doctor had prescribed a medicine to be taken that would kill the troublesome creatures, but Helena, had no idea what was to come. The medicine was a caramel brown syrupy substance, and she was to ingest it. She did, and an hour later, she felt a horrible pain deep inside her bowels, cramps, as if someone were stabbing her deep in her belly. She began moaning and bowled over to the floor. It was quiet. Her mother sat quietly on the couch, and her father in his recliner. They had not thought to turn on the TV for distraction, nor brought a cool towel for her forehead. She was to simply feel the pain, endure, until it was over, not knowing when that time would come or how long it would last. Did they know something she did not know? It remained silent. Perhaps if they had told her "it will only be a hour, dear," or " it's okay, you'll be fine," but they did not. It wasn't their style.

On the floor she had now begun speaking and groaning – pleading for help, comfort, anything.

"Daddy, it hurts...DAADDY IT HURTS!!! Owwww. Owwww." She twisted and writhed on the rough brown carpet.

Her father sat on the edge of his recliner, his hands clamped on his knees. He said nothing. He stared down at her, with only the smallest amount of sympathy. He remained still and simply waited.

Her moans continued. And then she stopped. Eventually. The pain was necessary for the medicine to work. Her mother followed suit and sat her on the couch when it was over. She soothed her some and then it was over. Just like that.

It wasn't always so, that she grew up in such indifferent complacence. Sometimes, at the dinner table, the family would chat, but mostly in defensive competitive banter, and this of course would usually end with someone feeling defeated. Helena sometimes felt ousted and would push her plate into the bowls on the dinner table causing them to clank together – a non verbal statement of angry protest. Then she would jump up from the table and retreat to her room, crying. Her father must have questioned this odd behavior for she caught him once at her bedroom window, staring in at her apologetically. She sat on the floor wiping her face of tears when she looked up and saw him. This made her angrier, for she did not like being seen crying much less being spied on.

They had a set of strict rules, that outside strangers might quite readily believe were odd. Helena was not allowed to watch any channel except public television, if they were allowed to watch TV at all. Her father called the TV – "The Idiot Box" – and limited TV time to only an hour or two a day. Helena's mother, both reverent and critical, enjoyed TV time, and felt it a fun time to be entertained and spend time with her child. Hence, while their father was at work, Helena and her mother would lounge in front of the TV and eat. They watched whatever Helena wanted and would laugh and talk. They kept this a secret from her father, and upon hearing the key in the front door, would jump and turn off the television, and sit at attention on the couch.

"Hi dad," Helena would murmur, holding open a book, pretending like she was reading.

"Hello," he would say, glancing around the home to ensure his authority.

Helena would never forget the day when her father caught them, when they were slow to turn off the television upon his arrival home. He became angry and pulled the TV, a large 1970's Zenith, from the wall socket and threw it in the backyard. He yelled at her mother for not following his orders and stormed out. Helena forgot whether they were able to use that same TV or whether they had to purchase another one. These details became fuzzy over the years. It was only years later, when Helena was a teenager, where her father became indifferent because he discovered he could not control others in that way. Helena used to curl up in front of the television and watch show after show for five hours straight. No one bothered her anymore, no one cared. Her father was usually holed up in his study, smoking his pipe and reading, in between teaching classes at the university, while her mother worked various shifts as a nurse. Her father seemed to turn things on their head, where he went from caring about things, maybe too much, to ignoring everyone and everything.

∾

Helena's father greeted her at the door when she arrived.

"Helena! Good to see you."

They hugged, and Mike Park stuck out his fist. She hit it with hers – a ritual they had done since she was a kid. He was wearing an old wool sweater with suede patches on the elbows and gray slacks. The hair left on his bald head was disheveled but stark black. He was getting thinner. Judith Park flew around the corner in a flurry of bright red.

"Helena!"

"Hi mom." She handed her a small package, a gold bracelet she had bought. "Happy birthday."

"Oh, thank you."

Helena drove them in her car to their favorite Chinese restaurant. They sat sipping tea.

"So, how's it going?" her father asked.

"Fine." She chatted about her work and how her cat got sick and she had to fork out $200 for the vet bill.

"$200?!" her mother exclaimed. "For a cat?"

"Why don't you get rid of that cat?" her father said.

"No. I love that cat. She's –"

"If you had someone, you wouldn't need the cat." Her mother said, adjusting the rings on her fingers.

"I don't *need* the cat, I *like* the cat."

It was odd hearing that from her mother, when she had told Helena once that she ought probably never marry because it would only be one headache after another.

"For twenty years, I put up with that man," her mother had told her, referring to her father. "It was a nightmare."

The food arrived. They ate in silence. Helena felt pressured to say something, obviously not about money, or the cat.

"I'm going to a leadership workshop. The company is sending me."

"Is that right?"

There it was. The remark that had always bothered Helena to no end. It was such a subtly diffusing comment, a conversation stopper, not receptive, not equalizing, but asserted a sense of their authority, and one that could only elicit an answer: yes or no. But usually, it was yes. Of course it was right, she just said it.

She looked at them. Her father had said it. But they were both equally guilty.

"Yeah."

"Where is it?" he continued, between bites of kung pao shrimp. He was curious now, nonchalant and relaxed.

"San Diego."

They seemed unimpressed, but not on purpose. Helena stared at them, trying to read them. She realized how inhuman she believed her parents were, that they didn't have feelings or thoughts. They were strong people, though not always perfect, but first generation immigrants who had done well for themselves. They were well-rounded, relaxed, comfortable, worldly. If they had worried at all about Helena in the past, they seemed to have recovered well. After all, she was doing well for herself, too. Finally.

"Now," her father piped in. "I hope you're not still smoking."

"I've cut down. Every once in a while." Helena lied. It was her one lasting flaw that needed to be corrected.

They went to a movie after dinner. Some popular martial arts action flick that her father wanted to see.

"You see, to me, that martial arts choreography is like dancing! It's like ballet!" her father exclaimed in the car on the way home.

Helena and her mother looked at each other and began laughing.

∞

"Hello, may I speak to Blythe Walker please?"

"One moment."

Elise tapped her pen on her desk blotter.

"Hello, Blythe Walker."

"Blythe, hello, this is Elise."

"Elise…how *are* you? What can I do for you?"

"I'm good. How are you?"

"Good."

"Well, I called because I wanted to bring something to your attention. Would you like to meet for lunch?"

Blythe Walker was a tall, thin woman with a neatly trimmed chocolate brown bob. She wore a beige suit with a green shirt and black pumps. Her mouth was colored in with a maroon red lipstick and she wore red rectangular horn-rimmed glasses. Elise dressed up that day, and wore a black pantsuit. They sat across from each other at the restaurant and ordered. Elise, a salad and water with lemon, and Blythe a club sandwich with ice tea.

"So what do I foresee for this momentous occasion?" asked Blythe.

"There is someone I know that I think you might want to bring to our paper."

"Really?"

"Yes. His name is Tom Overton, and although he's not from this area, he is someone we have found would be the perfect fit for our clerk position. The position just became available a few weeks ago."

"So we're talking relocation here?"

"Yes."

"Why haven't I already been notified?"

"Well, I…it's sort of something that I'm taking care of. He'll be under my wing."

"And you want me to hunt him for you."

"Please."

"Well, send me his resume."

"I have it for you. Here." She reached into her bag and pulled out a sheet of paper. She slid it across the table.

Blythe picked it up and read it.

"Hmmm, seems like a bright one."

"He is, we would really like him to join our team."

"Well…OK."

Inside, Elise was doing cartwheels. That was it. The operation was a go.

"One thing, he's got some articles on Chicago. com. He also has this exact resume on the Hireme. com Job Board. If you could tell him that we saw those articles and his resume and would like to hire him, don't mention that you and I had a meeting."

Blythe was still scanning the resume.

"Mm, hmm. Alright. Chicago.com?"

"Yes."

Blythe took out a pen and made a note on the resume.

"I'll get right on it."

Well, thought Elise. That wasn't so hard. After a rather long trek in trying to get Elise hired somewhere, Blythe and Elise became rather close. Blythe was good at giving Elise tips in interviewing skills, securing interviews and general career management. Elise was grateful and took her out to lunch every once in a while. They found they had both gone to the same university, five years apart, and had a common interest in Italian graphic design from the 20s and 30s. Blythe had told Elise once that she had "good people skills."

"It's an important skill to have," Blythe had said. "And if I can tell you one thing: you always want to go up, never down."

6

The ousting, to Helena and Elise's surprise, had been relatively easy.

Chester Mills, the news clerk at the Sun Valley Herald, received his assignment and called Helena the next day like clockwork. Throughout the rest of that day and the next morning, he left numerous messages with Helena's secretary, mainly asking for an in-person appointment to interview her for the Sun Valley Herald. Helena made sure to tell Anastasia to hold all her calls, and take messages, that she would be busy for the next few days.

Then one day, Anastasia buzzed her.

Helena pushed her caller button.

"Helena, it's this reporter from the Herald, he says it's really important that he talk to you."

"OK, let him through."

Chester couldn't believe his luck. Finally, he breathed. He wiped his forehead and leaned back in his chair.

"Yes, this is Helena Park, how can I help you?"

"Yes, Ms. Park, I uh, my name is Chester Mills from the Sun Valley Herald? I left some messages regarding an interview."

"OK."

"Well, I would like to know if I could meet you in person. I've been assigned to write a profile of you as one of our portraits of success," he said. He wasn't sure what kind of person she was, having ignored him these last couple of days. Perhaps she was just very busy. That was believable.

"I'm afraid I don't have the time to meet you in person, Ches - is it Chester?

"Yes, ma'am."

"Chester. Could we conduct a phone interview?"

"Oh, well, I'd really rather meet you in person, but if that's all we can get, then that would fine."

"Great, I'm going to have to call you back at the end of the day."

"Well, actually, my deadline is today."

"Oh, alright, well, then, fire away."

Chester breathed another sigh of relief, tinged with exasperation. He pulled up to his desk and leaned forward with his fingers floating above the keyboard, poised to take notes.

He began the interview. Helena flubbed some of the information. Then she corrected it, then she flubbed it again. What's wrong with this woman, Chester thought. She sounds drunk.

At the same time of the interview, Elise began sending e-mails to Chester reminding him of his deadline and asking why he was still in the newsroom when he should be out interviewing Helena.

Chester kept seeing the e-mail message icon in the corner of his computer screen during his interview. The first couple of times he put Helena on hold to answer them, at which time Helena promptly hung up. When he returned to her and found the line dead, he had to call her back and go through her secretary again. After the second time, Helena informed Anastasia that she was leaving for the day.

"Take my messages. Thanks." She handed Anastasia some folders for filing before locking her office shut and leaving the building.

"Unbelievable!" Chester said to himself when he had learned she had actually left him mid-interview. Now what? He was desperate. Make something up, no, that was the first cardinal rule of journalism, it had to be accurate and it had to be based in fact. It was now 4:30. He had half an hour to write a credible piece. He looked up Helena Park on the Internet and found an article about her in a local business newsletter. He took some information from it. He had fleshed out the article just enough for the 400 word limit.

He would have been fine had he taken care of two things: attributed the information he took from the newsletter, and *not* told his editor, Elise, what he had done. He had always been one to give too much information. Another mistake: he sent this information to her by e-mail.

Chester Mills was a transplant from Ohio. He had a blond military buzz cut that stood up stiffly with gel revealing a slight widow's peak. Even though it was blond, you could still see flakes of dandruff scattered across the fuzzy landscape of his hair. His cheeks were spattered with acne, red from constant picking. It was a bad habit that had developed due to nervous energy since he started working at the Herald. He had gotten notice of being hired for the job of news clerk at the Sun Valley Herald straight out of college. He had dabbled in writing editorials for his university newspaper and creative writing. After he had gotten the call from the Herald, he had run straight to his room, flung himself on his bed and screamed into his pillow while kicking his legs wildly on the mattress. It lasted about a minute. His dream was to write for the National Review, but he knew he had to pay his dues first. His school editorials focused on things from the mundane to the universal. Whatever happened to catch his fancy at the time. The one he was most proud of was about his disagreement that certain professors encouraged students to consider the merit of attending student protests, especially if it had to do with improving university services. If others were compelled to attend class, why should those who wished to attend a demonstration (which, on principle, he was not particularly in agreement with anyway, considering them disruptive and useless) be encouraged to do so? He had brought up the issue with one of his professors who taught American Government.

"Well, Chester, this is a university, and you are all college students. I encourage the freedom for each student to make his or her own decision whether or not to attend class, and many let me know ahead of time where they will be going, so I generally let it go," explained his professor, Dr. Griffin.

Chester knew the real reason why the majority of his professors "let it go" – they secretly encouraged student demonstrations, believing it was free speech. Another professor had responded that he believed in the "healthy exchange of ideas." Chester had left the classroom, scoffing. They were all die-hard liberals. Hence, the editorial.

When Chester had heard he had gotten the job at the Herald, he had started packing immediately, hooked a U-Haul trailer to his green Ford Escort and headed to California. He had started as soon as he arrived, and embarked on a career path that had lasted, until now, up to a year.

Elise received Chester's piece just in time, at 5 p.m. Staffers were packing up and heading home. The night shifters were slowly trickling in. She was saying goodbye and hello simultaneously. Elise had also received all of Chester's e-mails. It took her a while to put two and two together and realize what he had done.

Had someone had x-ray vision they would see the wheels spinning inside Elise's head and the mouse running on the wheel. She edited the piece quickly and sent it over to the copy desk. The day had been a long one. She was eager to leave and sleep on what had just occurred. She was beginning to feel a twinge of guilt, but in actuality, everything had gone as planned. She didn't realize how easy it could be to mess up someone's life.

∾

Chester walked into the newsroom two days later at 8 a.m. sharp. Elise was waiting for him at her desk. Chester turned to her and smiled nervously.

"Good morning," he said.

"Good morning."

"Chester, before you get started, let's talk."

She led the way to the small conference room and sat down with him.

"I got a call yesterday from the CEO at Precise Communications. They own Precise Business Weekly, a local newsletter. They said that you had copied some information from their profile on Helena Park from the January edition of the newsletter. Is that true?"

Chester's eyes grew watery.

"Yes. But I –"

"This is a very serious offense, Chester. They could sue us for plagiarism."

"I'm truly sorry, Elise. I had such a hard time getting through to Ms. Park, as I told you in the e-mail, and –"

"Yes, I know, but sometimes Chester you have to be able to take initiative. Why didn't you go straight to her office?"

"I thought I should set an appointment first."

"Well, I'm sorry Chester, but we're going to have to let you go."

Chester sighed. Then he began crying. Elise felt it now – guilt.

"Listen, Chester, you're still young. It's OK."

"Can't you give me another chance? It won't happen again, I promise."

"I'm sorry, Chester. We can't take any more chances. You'll find a box in the warehouse where you can put your things."

She stood up and stuck out her hand. Chester stood up and wiped his eyes quickly. Then he shook her hand, and looking down, left the conference room.

Elise went to her desk and sat down. Mission accomplished – so far. She had yet to find out how Blythe was doing in her request to recruit Tom. They had to notify him, and then get him relocated. After that, he would have his first day on the job and get situated before anything could transpire between him and Helena, as Helena had projected. They had to do all this while keeping their cool, as if it were business as usual. They had to go about this in just enough secrecy that is allowed by the mysterious workings of the hiring process. For it is, and could be, quite complicated by nature, which is what made these loopholes to begin with. Did anyone who had been fired before, ever really know the real reason why they had been fired? Could politics so monopolize a situation that no one could ever really know what happened and why? Elise had just performed her first real power play by taking advantage of her position. Ethically and morally she could now officially be seen as being corrupt. Why was she always letting Helena talk her into things? This was by far the most outrageous thing she had done. But actually, it wasn't. They had never really conspired about anything before. It wasn't that she was a bad person, not at all. In fact, she was bright, funny, and personable. They hadn't been friends that long, only a few years. But what she liked the most was just talking to her over drinks and cigarettes, even though Helena had given up alcohol years ago.

She knew deep inside that she couldn't blame Helena.

Elise felt as though she deserved a reward. But she also felt as though she should be punished. The oddest thing about how she felt though, was her ambivalence. She felt both drunk with power and red with shame.

∾

Tom Overton was up late. He had only one more day of training in L.A. and then it was back home to Chicago. He was busy looking over the paper-work he had received from the sessions. Not too bad, he thought, I can handle this. Each day he felt better and better about the job. Now that he had the great job, all that was missing was a girlfriend. He wasn't one to pine away after broken relation-ships, but he had his fair share of nostalgia. What he missed most was waking up late on weekends and going out for breakfast, drinking lots of coffee and then catching an exhibit at the museum. He missed waking up next to her in the morning. He would wake her gently with a kiss on the mouth. She would stir and then slowly open her eyes and smile.

He shook his head and went to the mini refrig-erator. He popped open a beer bottle from a pack he had bought earlier and took a sip. He was start-ing to pine, and he didn't want to pine. He turned on the television and sat on the couch. Great. Jeopardy. The College edition.

What many would not know about Tom Overton was that he had once been addicted to cocaine. He had not had any cocaine in a long time, and he considered himself off the drug. It became a habit with him briefly and then on and off over the years during law school. He had spent a fair amount of time on the drug, and had several episodes of acute psychosis. This psychosis had caused him at one time to stay indoors, with a baseball bat, for fear of intruders coming in to invade his home and raid it for drugs. At one time of this unfortunate circumstance, Tom Overton had been watching the game show Jeopardy and had very distinctly heard the host Alex Trebek and the contestants playing the game. He had stared at the television, eyes wide as he slowly became enveloped with fear. He froze, as his eyes darted back and forth to the contestants unassuming faces, the categories and back to Alex Trebek. He became suspicious of their joviality and smug knowledge. What it was that Tom Overton had heard was that these contestants and the host Alex Trebek were very specifically talking *about* and *to* him and his life. They were mocking him.

Tom had not thought about this for a long time. He watched the channel for a while and waited for any sign of parallel similarity with the game categories, the contestants, or the host, to his life right now as he knew it. He strained to listen. He kept careful watch. There were none. It was an innocent game show. Precocious Ivy League college students were winning money. He was fine.

It was then that Tom decided to check his e-mail. He turned on his laptop computer and opened up his Inbox. There were several messages, some newsletters, he had unwittingly signed up for on some site he had crossed when Web surfing on numerous occasions. They were so numerous that he had forgotten what they were for. Mostly prerequisites to gaining access to information he was looking for on a certain site. From a scholarship search company to health newsletters, he enjoyed seeing the bold lettering of new messages rolling into view, but then felt disappointed when none were of any significance. He had gotten one message, from a friend.

> **How's the job? Teresa and I broke up. Life sucks now. What about you? Sara keeps asking about you. I gave her your email. Hope that's ok? You missed something cool. John had an exhibit of his work. He actually sold some stuff.**
> **Take it ez-**
> **LG**

LG was Lowell Godfrey. Tom knew him only briefly, but they immediately became close friends. They had the same taste in music, art and books. Lowell was a part-time musician and collected instruments. He came from an uptight, New

England family, and he had moved to Chicago to escape taking over his father's cigar business. He and Tom had met at a party of a mutual friend. He went out with a million girlfriends in a month, but always complained that he was lonely. Tom couldn't seem to help him out in that regard. All he could do was listen to him and be a friend. And Lowell liked to talk, a lot. Tom thought for a while, and looked through his newsletters. Then he wrote back.

> **Job is good. Still in training, but life's OK here. I miss everyone. Good for John. Tell him I said Hey.**
> **Sorry about you and Teresa. No one here for me, yet. But I'm looking. It's ok that you gave Sara my email. Not much else happening. Come up for a visit. Or hopefully I'll make it back soon.**
> **Tom**

Tom clicked the Send button. He surfed the Web for a while, mainly looking on job sites for freelance writers. He still wanted to pursue writing to some degree, whether it was an elusive dream or not. He pulled up some short stories he had been working on and tried to evaluate them. One thing was that he wished he had someone who would read them and tell him what they thought without being too judgmental. He couldn't think of anyone. He couldn't bring himself to show them to Lowell, because in actuality, Lowell had a competitive streak that made him, actually, quite mean.

He sat and stared absently into cyberspace for a while, and then closed all his programs. He did all this just before an email message popped into his Inbox titled: **Job Offer**.

7

As Tom rolled out of bed the next day, he would still not know the larger workings of the universe that surrounded him. For him, it was just another ordinary day where he might possibly be confronted by a certain number of situations, some good, some bad, but overall they would constitute the continued experience that he would dub his life.

Helena would light her first cigarette of the day wondering what Tom was doing at that very moment – for she was sure she was in love with him and couldn't wait to hear the news from him one day very soon where he would ask to speak to her, and accept the job offer in L.A. that the headhunter had hunted him for. She would suddenly stop and think though, was there a chance that he would not accept the offer? Perhaps he was comfortable in Chicago and did not want to move? She thought for a moment and panicked briefly. She would have Elise call him directly and cajole him into accepting it. Elise would call, in addition to Blythe Walker, and hopefully the pressure of the two would break him. Why wouldn't he accept? Of course he would.

When Elise Rudolph arrived at work she put in a call to Blythe for an update on Tom Overton. She was delighted to hear that the job offer had been made via e-mail and regular mail, but they had yet to hear a response.

"Great," Elise said. "Thank you."

"Sure," Blythe answered.

"Once you hear from him, would you notify me ASAP?"

"Absolutely."

Elise thanked her again and hung up.

∞

Tom strolled into the office and took his usual seat in the conference room. Gerard was there, along with the other new hires. Helena walked in minutes later. Tom stared at her lithe, petite figure but made sure not to let his gaze linger. He pulled out his paperwork and pretended to study. Helena had decided to wear her hair down that day. It framed her face with dark, loose waves. She saw Tom and immediately became nervous. Her stomach began to ache. She swallowed hard. Keep it together, she kept saying to herself.

"We're going to have a brief session today, so you'll probably be happy to know that you'll get to go home, or rather, to your respective hotel rooms, early," Gerard began.

They went over some more basics about the company's expectations and the hard and fast rules of consultants. They did some team exercises and then called it a day at 1 p.m. No lunch break. But they were free to go.

Tom felt relieved. He wanted to go back to the hotel room and take a nap. His flight left back to Chicago tomorrow morning at 8 a.m.

Helena watched Tom's every move as he gathered up his things and prepared to leave. She hoped this wouldn't be the last time she would see him. His hands picked up the papers and shuffled them together as he put them in his briefcase. He stood up, reached for his jacket and threw it on his lean frame. Then he ran his hand through his hair on the right side and turned and made his way out of the conference room. Helena stared at his retreating back, closed her eyes and breathed in deeply before exhaling. She stood up quickly and turned off the television where they had just shown a video presentation.

She would soon be with him, she hoped.

∽

"I can't believe we pulled it off," Helena remarked happily.

Elise was silent.

"Be nice to him once he gets there, OK? I mean, go easy on the nonsense that goes on where you work. Let him grow and thrive," Helena continued.

"Anyone can do reviews Helena. He's just a news clerk, he'll have time to learn. I can assure you that," Elise paused. "So when are you going to make your move?"

"Well, I figure once he tells me he's leaving, I can give him my card or tell him to get in touch with me when he gets here. Or, I can ask him where the job is and he'll say Sun Valley Herald and I'll say, 'Hey, my good friend is an editor there, why don't we all go have lunch sometime?'"

"It's just so…unlike you, getting sappy over some guy."

"I wouldn't call it sappy – I think it's fate. He interviewed for the job at Advent for a reason. I just hope he's nothing like Shawn"

Shawn, who was five years her senior, and Helena had been an item when Helena was in college. She was a sophomore when she met him and then broke up officially after only six months. They then got back together in her last year of college.

"That was the most twisted relationship you have ever had."

"I'm way past that now. Granted, that was a doomed relationship, but I ran away when he wanted me to meet his parents. I just totally ran away from it all."

"Because he couldn't commit to you."

"So I did the right thing."

"After so much pain and suffering."

Helena finished her ice cream. She paid the bill, a thank you dinner for Elise, and they both gathered their purses and left the restaurant.

"Thanks for everything you've done, Elise, I mean it."

"Yeah, well, I'll be expecting wedding bells after this," she looked at Helena and smiled.

"There's always hope for miracles," said Helena.

∾

Tom woke up and looked at the clock. 6:30 p.m.

He picked up the room service menu and ordered a burger and fries.

He took off his shirt, stretched and turned on the television. He flipped through the channels and landed on a channel with L.A. Law reruns. He watched it for a while, and then changed it to CNN.

His food finally arrived and he ate, dreading the flight out tomorrow, only because it was so early. He was feeling it, traveling had already become tiresome. He would probably have trouble getting to sleep that night because of his long nap, so he would be tired tomorrow. He could always sleep on the plane. This consoled him, so he stopped worrying about it.

He thought about checking his e-mail, but didn't feel like it. What's a day without checking? He sat back in bed in his boxers and watched TV until 1 a.m. then he fell asleep.

The next morning, he woke up late. He jumped out of bed and began to get ready. He decided to wear a baseball cap so he didn't have to worry about his hair and threw on a pair of jeans and a t-shirt. He pulled on a pair of Pumas and got his suitcase together along with his carry on messenger bag. He hurried down the hall to the elevator to meet his taxi outside.

It was a long but pleasant drive to the L.A. airport. He felt relieved going home and back to his apartment in Chicago. So that was L.A. Nothing special.

The airport was crowded as he rolled his suitcase to the gate to board the plane. When he arrived he checked the TV screens to make sure there were no delays or cancellations. L.A. to Chicago. One stopover in Phoenix. Everything seemed to be set as scheduled. He sat down and leaned back comfortably in his seat. He rubbed his eyes and yawned. He contemplated getting a cup of coffee at the airport coffee bar. He wondered if it might be easier on his body if he just slept on the plane. He decided to stay where he was and sleep on the plane. He sat and watched the people around him. A kid was sitting across from him playing games on his cell phone. Men and women in suits walked briskly past him. A couple of young college students were sitting nearby wearing huge backpacks and hiking shoes. He was sorry that he wasn't able to take some time to travel when he had the time, somewhere between college and law school. He had taken a family vacation to Southeast Asia, which was great, but he really wanted to visit Europe. Maybe go backpacking with a girlfriend or a close friend. Now he was too busy strapped down with working the daily grind to pay off loans. The idea pissed him off, and he quickly tried to think of other things.

He began to get restless waiting to board the plane. Luckily, the PA announced his flight and he stood up, took his suitcase and walked quickly to the gate to check in and board his flight.

Once he settled in, he waited anxiously for the plane to take off. When it finally did, several minutes later, the stewardess began to walk up the aisle with the drink cart. He waited, and got a tomato juice. He drained it and then curled up with his pillow and tried to fall asleep. He stayed awake for a good half hour and then finally nodded off.

When he awoke, he ordered a coffee. He looked out at the clouds, while listening to his iPod and sipped his coffee. He began to wake up and felt a lot less cranky. His system started to settle down and he felt calm.

Time passed steadily and the pilot announced that they had arrived in Phoenix. Tom took off his headphones and straightened his seat, as directed. Then the passengers disembarked only to have to wait in the Phoenix station for what ended up being about an hour. Tom started the whole ritual over again when he embarked on the plane. He was starting to get tired and wondered whether this job was really worth it.

8

~

Tom threw his bag on the couch and went to check his phone messages.

In the three days that he had been gone, he received three messages. One from his mother, one from his father (they were divorced), and one from his sister. They were all asking how he was since he had not bothered to call any of them since he had moved to Chicago. It had been about one month.

Just at that moment, the phone rang.

"Hello."

"Tom, dear, are you OK? My God, where have you been?"

"Mom, I'm fine. I just got back from a business trip in L.A. I got a job. I have an apartment, I'm fine."

"Do you know what we had to do to get your number? We had to track down your friend in Chicago, Rose had the number, and –"

"Yes, mom, I'm sorry."

"You have to give us your cell phone number too – and your email. You changed everything."

"My cell is 773-970-2917. And my email is Toverton at Advent dot com. That's my work email."

"How's Chicago, dear?"

"Great, Chicago is great."

"Have you talked to Rose?"

"No, I'm going to call her after I'm off with you."

"How's work?"

"Good, so far. I've been in training."

"What are you doing? I hope you've started to practice."

"No. I'm consulting again."

"Oh." Her voice was tinged with slight disappointment. Then she started.

"What is so hard about finding a job at a firm? I just don't understand. You have great education, you –"

"Mom, I'm hanging up. I'll talk to you later…"

"Good bye dear."

Tom hung up the phone.

He decided he would rather email his sister, and his father. But first, he would need to order a pizza and have a beer.

He looked around his apartment. He felt alone. He didn't like feeling this way because he started to get paranoid. He thought that maybe he should have moved in with a roommate. At least then he would have someone to talk to.

He sat on the couch. What was really wrong? Did he feel frustrated? Afraid? Angry?

His thoughts immediately turned to his last relationship. She started to feel suffocated, which is what she told him. He wasn't sure if he was really in love with her, but rather more that he needed her to fill up this empty space he felt when he was alone. He knew of friends that had someone they were together with almost every night. Why not she and he?

As he sat and thought, he began to realize – he pushed her too soon. But what about these stories where people get married in four months? Why couldn't that happen with him? Not that he really wanted to get married. He wanted the security of the marriage, without the legality of it. The legalities of marriage made him nervous. It was so final - a contract between a couple's love and God and the state. But he wanted someone's devotion and commitment.

He held his head. He was tired of thinking. He wondered where his pizza was. He was starving.

He opened up his laptop and plugged it in. As he heard his stomach growl, he waited for the computer to start up. He opened his Inbox and watched the emails roll in. Then it caught his eye: **Job Offer.** What? He thought. He clicked it open and read its contents.

Dear Tom,

My name is Blythe Walker and I am a headhunter at SMP Recruiters, Inc. We have found your resume on

HireMe.com and would like to offer you a job in the publishing field.

You have expressed interest in this field and we would like to know if you would come in for an interview for News Clerk at the Sun Valley Herald in Sun Valley, CA. This opening will only be available for a limited time so we urge you to respond quickly.

You may reply to this e-mail or call me at 310-740-4367.

Thank you.

Sincerely,
Blythe Walker SMP Recruiters, Inc.

Tom stared at the screen and read the message again. Then a third time, and a fourth time. He was absolutely stunned that something like this could have happened to him. Was this for real? If so, what luck! He looked forward to the idea of being in California. He would have to think fast. He knew he should have checked his email yesterday.

His buzzer rang. It was the pizza.

Tom opened the door to a scrawny teenager with a scar on his cheek.

"Hey," they both acknowledged each other.

Tom paid for the pizza and closed the door.

He sat in front of his laptop and pulled a gooey slice from the box. He bit into it with great satisfaction. After finishing one piece, he pulled another out and set it on a paper plate on the coffee table. He wiped his fingers on his pants and then turned to his laptop and hit the Reply button. Then he began typing.

> **Dear Blythe,**
> **Thank you for your message.**

He deleted "message."

> **Thank you for your offer.**
> **I accept your**

He deleted the first sentence.

> **I accept your offer for News Clerk at the Sun Valley Herald.**
> **I thank you very much for this offer and I look forward to hearing details.**
> **I am currently located in Chicago, IL. Are relocation expenses covered?**
> **Thank you again.**
> **Sincerely,**
> **Tom Overton**

He read it over and over and wondered if he should ask about salary. Maybe he would wait. He decided to modify the message.

**I thank you very much for this offer
and I look forward to hearing details.
I would be happy to come in for an
interview.
Thank you again.
Sincerely,
Tom Overton**

He left it at that and clicked Send. Now he would have to wait for her response. That was one thing about e-mail, it allowed you to edit your message over and over, a luxury one did not have when speaking, but waiting for a response could be agonizing for the impatient.

He went through his other e-mails. Lowell had not yet written back. There was a message from Sara, one of his former roommates. He read it and replied quickly. He was preoccupied with what had just happened and its possibilities that he paid little attention to anything else at that moment. He began doing some research online about the Sun Valley Herald. He would have to fly out again, but he didn't care. He was excited about this prospect. He couldn't wait to get started. He wondered who he might be working with. From his experience writing for Chicago.com, editors were tough but respected you as long as you worked hard and met the deadlines. He had done most of his work with them through telecommuting, while dropping

into the office every once in a while. He wondered what his job as "news clerk" would entail.
It sounded like something he could handle. He
would have to wait and see.

9

~

It was late, past 2 a.m. and Helena's thoughts were running through her head and wouldn't stop. They kept careening into trains that connected to a track that split into forks, past her window mantle and the plants on the sill. She stared at them. It was as if her thoughts were jumping out of her.

It soon became tiresome. She began thinking of the past, again. Was she really healed? Could she ever get over this?

She had moved to Los Angeles with a boyfriend, Lenny, to look for a job and because she was bored. They had moved into an apartment and she had gotten a job doing administrative work at a cruise line. She had then gotten involved with, Byron, who helped her recover after she had split from Lenny, an alcoholic with a bad temper.

The one thing she had noticed right away with Byron was the enormous faith he had in people. He was thin with sandy hair and blue eyes that always looked moist, as if he had been holding back tears for most of his life.

She can't say that she had the wherewithal at the time to judge that situation. She was fogged up from emotional pain and a waning drug habit that could only be called "tragic" for someone of her stature. She was desperate in her desire to be desired. A fallen princess. A deer lost in the head-lights. She could now say with a decent measure of confidence that she was simply "chemically imbalanced."

She had the epiphany after Byron left. She wasn't sure why he left. She was too messed up to understand. He was seven years her senior, and recently divorced. She wrote him a letter, in her typical fashion, ruminating about their relation-ship. She received one back. One page, with a line that would stick with her forever: "You will always have a place in my heart." Anyway, he had told her, in the fog of one evening of drinking several bottles of wine, "I can't make you any promises."

It was then that she fell into the pit of depres-sion, so dark, so painful, she had to call him for help. She saw fire and demons, darkness and death. She cried, drank, fell asleep, and woke up and did it all over again. When she found out he had met someone after only two weeks, she was crushed. She had been so easy to forget. She knew deep down inside that he did not know her well enough to really fall in love with her. She did not

let him know her. She was scared. That was, ulti-
mately, what led him astray.

So she remembered the good times. He had
helped her set up her new apartment after Lenny
had left. She had found an apartment right
around the corner from his place. She was nursing some serious wounds, but vowed to start over
again by moving into the slightly run-down, but
halfway livable four apartment bungalow complex.
It had brown wall-to-wall carpet, the thin, lumpy
kind that wouldn't improve with any amount of
professional shampooing. The kitchen cupboards
were ugly and musty. The bathroom showerhead
spouted a fierce, fire hose spray that bruised even
the toughest, calloused skin on the heel of your
foot. The limestone deposits had encrusted the
holes embedding themselves deeply into the noz-
zle. Byron had come over with a huge wrench to
help her replace it. It was quite a feat, but afterwards, she had a decent shower spray to pass her
days with.

She added a fish tank to the living room. Byron
had lent her a metal tool shelf, which she doubled
as a bookcase. It was the type of shelf you found in
a garage that stored things like paint cans, power
tools, boxes of nails, golf balls, fishing line. She had
pulled out the old fish tank that she had received
as a gift from a friend on her birthday years ago.
The goldfish she later placed in the tank seemed
happy, and she added a blue light on top to reflect

the blue iridescence of a handful of polished rocks placed on the bed of blue gravel. She and Byron sat in the living room where she had spread out a straw mat to cover the deplorable carpeting. With no other furniture, except a small table where her TV and VCR sat, they sat on the floor in the dark watching the fish. It was beautiful. They sat and watched it for a long time. Then Byron turned to Helena and asked her what she was going to do from then on, now that Lenny was out of her life. She didn't want to answer him. She felt sick and twisted inside, uneasy and miserable. She turned to him and smiled, "Just be with you, I suppose." He wanted in on her life, wanted a part of it, but she wouldn't let that happen. Then she had tried to kiss him, but he had pulled away and sighed. He stretched out on the floor in silence, watching the fish tank. She decided not to disturb him.

A few months after she had settled in, she still had no couch. The old, yellowing smoke-stained curtains covering the windows didn't open, the runners were stuck. The windows were covered in wrought-iron caging. The front door with its heavy wrought iron gate slammed shut like a prison door every time you entered or exited the house. Helena got used to the Hispanic kids running around the building in the apartment below, screaming and pounding the cracked asphalt, slamming their wrought iron doors that led to their apartments.

Then there was the day when through the kitchen window, which she at first had liked for not having a screen, a cockroach the size of a baby's fist came flying in just after dusk. It had landed on the wall above the television settling in among some of Helena's own drawings which she had framed. She had screamed and grabbed a bottle of bathroom bleach cleaner and sprayed the entire wall only to chase it around the room and have it land in the kitchen wastebasket. After unsuccessfully trying to smash it with the end of a broomstick, she maniacally sprayed into the wastebasket until the bottom quarter was filled with bleach. Overturning bits of garbage, she finally found it, on its back, drowned in bleach, dead at last.

The apartment had not come with a refrigerator. After perusing the classifieds, Byron had taken her to a yard sale in the neighborhood to buy one. When they had arrived at the sale, an old crusty man with a baseball cap and graying stubble wobbled out to the yard to show it to them. Byron had borrowed his friend's truck and they hauled the thing into the back. It cost $75. When she finally got it up to her kitchen, the bottom screen kept falling off, the freezer had a wooden door on the inside, and upon closer inspection one could see that it had been painted over with brown paint. As the months went by, the freezer proved virtually useless as it froze over with ice into a solid block. It was a disaster.

The bedroom was the only redeeming feature about the place. It had a walk-in closet, and everything seemed to fit into place. She had placed the bookshelf near the doorway, the bed in the corner across from it, the desk in the corner across from the foot of the bed and a small crate made into an altar was in the last corner near the closet. It was perfectly square and a tidy cave of a haven. An added bonus was that the curtains opened, and there was no wrought iron gating on the window. She had a view of the ancient historical artifacts that came in the form of the beautifully designed Victorian-style houses across the street that were commonplace in Echo Park. One in particular, was a bright yellow house with a large porch and bright windows. The setting sun in mid-afternoon would bounce off the paint creating shades of dark and light. She would stare out at that house, imagining what might be going on inside. She imagined an old lady circling the dining room in a walker waiting for tea time while the television buzzed in the background, the smell of aspercreme and stewed carrots permeating throughout the house. She would be overseeing a group of her grandchildren who would be running in and out of the rooms and up and down the stairs.

The bedroom was her sanctuary. She did a lot of reading in her twin size futon and spent many late night hours on the computer, exploring what was then the new World Wide Web and doing research. She and Byron would sleep in before getting up to have brunch in Chinatown. Her meditation altar in the corner beset with candles and incense took her to what she believed to be unexpected levels of higher consciousness at the time. It was also where she and Byron made love. She remembered the night when he had first hinted to her that she needed "help."

She remembered the outside of the building, too. Just outside the bedroom window, on the building, there were iron numbers nailed to the wall, indicating the address. Next to the numbers was a decorative symbol, an object made of metal in the shape of a circle with shards erupting from all sides, most resembling, upon first glance, a sun.

Before the relationship with Byron ended, he had brought her a potted plant one day that would only be awaiting a sad, early death due to sheer negligence. One day he had visited her and she noticed him glancing at it in all its browned dry glory only to look away, as if she had failed some test. Perhaps she had, but at the time she did not know it. The end was near, she could feel him pulling away. Looking back now, she wished she could go back in time and do things differently, but of course, she couldn't. This was difficult for her to accept. She had failed to see all the signs.

He had angrily taken back all the books he had lent her, storming around her apartment looking for them while she sat and cried at the kitchen table.

When he left, she got up to look at herself in the mirror. Her skin was smooth and white. Her eyes puffy and red from crying. She could think of nothing else to do but take a good look at herself in the mirror. She couldn't understand what she saw. It baffled her. How could someone so innocent looking feel so awful? Or was it innocence she saw? Perhaps it was just a mask of piety, learned from growing up in two worlds: her own skewed perception of life vs. reality as the world presented it.

Byron had told her that he liked her because she had qualities that his ex-wife did not. She didn't want to guess what those qualities were, because she imagined that these were qualities that she didn't like about herself.

Helena squelched her pain by getting out of bed and lighting a cigarette. She wanted to quit smoking and immediately was reminded of her weakness in not being able to. She puffed away and turned on the television. She took out her journal from her desk and went and sat on the couch. She began writing furiously, at first about not being able to sleep, and then her thoughts veered toward Tom and she began to relax. She closed her eyes and dreamed about him. She drew a picture of him and her in her journal, like a schoolgirl, she drew hearts and rainbows floating in between the cartoon-like images of she and Tom. The drawing made her feel better; it gave her a release. When she was done, she stared at the drawing and smiled. She began to relax and felt sleepy. She closed her journal and stretched out on the couch. Thank God tomorrow is Saturday, she thought. She drifted off to sleep amidst the glow of the fluorescent light of the television.

∞

Blythe Walker was having a bad day. Her supervisor had dumped all this extra work on her and it was 4:00 p.m. She would have to stay late. She hated staying late. She was flipping through a file, when the phone rang.

"Blythe Walker."

"Hello, Ms. Walker, my name is Tom Overton. I received an e-mail from you regarding a position with the Sun Valley Herald?"

Blythe was silent for a minute. She was searching her mind asking herself where that name sounded familiar.

"Tom Overton? Can you hold for a moment?"

She pulled up her database and found his name. Then it came back to her. Elise. News Clerk. Interview.

She pushed the hold button.

"Yes, Tom, hello. The editor at the Herald would like to meet with you for an interview. When is a good day for you?"

"Any day, except, I have to fly out. I can make it in next week on Friday. I think I can ask for that day off."

"Okay, Friday at 3 p.m.? What I'll do, Tom, is I will ask the editor who will be meeting with you to call and confirm."

"Okay, that sounds good."

They both hung up. Blythe picked up the phone and called Elise. She wasn't there so she left a message. Then she turned back to her computer and was reminded of all the files she had to get through. She sighed heavily and got to work.

∾

Elise was in the hallway talking with a fellow editor when Blythe had left her message. They were just chewing the fat, wasting a little time before the crunch of deadline. Elise was munching on a South Beach Diet peanut butter protein bar while her co-worker, Ed, sipped a Starbucks coffee. Elise leaned against the wall with stooped shoulders, a sign she was tired. Then something unexpected happened. Ed suddenly asked about Chester.

"What happened?"

Elise stopped chewing.

"Oh, well, he took some information from another source, without attributing it. It was a classic case of plagiarism."

"Really?" replied Ed. "Too bad. He was a nice kid."

"Yeah, well, things happen." She looked at her watch. "Listen, I've got to get back to the desk. It was nice chatting with you Ed, I'll see you around."

"Sure."

Elise got to her desk and threw the wrapper of her protein bar away in the trash. She picked up her phone to check her messages. When she got the message from Blythe, she stiffened. This was it. She jotted down the number of Tom Overton. Then she hung up the phone and was about to punch in the number when she realized that it would probably be safer if she called after most of the staff had gone home and from an enclosed office. She had her reasons. Staffers could be awfully nosy, and she didn't want any gossip to start flying about how this new clerk got hired.

She watched the clock carefully, and went about her daily duties. Finally, the clock hit 5:30 and she went outside to the break area and dialed from her cell phone.

"Hello."

"Hello, may I speak to Tom Overton?"

"Yes, speaking."

"Tom, this is Elise Rudolph from the Sun Valley Herald. How are you?"

"Hello. I'm good, thanks. How are you?"

"Good, fine. So it looks as if you are able to come meet with us about the news clerk position that just opened up. We're looking forward to meeting you."

"Yes, I'm looking forward to meeting you, too."

"Well, it looks as if next Friday the 12th at 3 p.m. will do."

"Great. I really appreciate this opportunity, thank you so much." Tom sat down on his bed and played with his hair.

"You're very welcome. So then we will see you on Friday. Do you have any questions?"

Tom thought fast. How would he get there?

"Well, can I have the address of your offices so I know where to go once I land?"

"Absolutely…that might help, huh?" She smiled. "Our address is 5709 W. Palmer, Sun Valley, CA."

He quickly jumped up and fumbled for a pen in his bag. Then he jotted it down on a piece of newspaper. He tore it free and set it on his kitchen table.

"Ok, thank you, I will see you then."

"Great! Good bye Tom."

"Good bye."

Elise tapped her phone to hang up and let out a heavy sigh. This whole thing was really beginning to drain her energy.

Tom tapped the hang up button on his phone and copied the address into his organizer. He would have to find a place to stay. He had a distant cousin who he remembered lived in the area, but he didn't feel he knew her well enough to stay with her. She had a family and kids, and he didn't want to put that kind of pressure on her. He didn't want to make a burden of himself. He also felt more comfortable staying in a hotel. He liked the privacy and the freedom to do what he wanted.

He began searching on the Internet to look for accommodations in Sun Valley, CA for Friday the 12th. One night.

∾

After hearing Tom's request, and granting it, Gerard wondered how good this Tom Overton kid would be. Secretly, he had slightly disagreed with the decision to hire him, but the final decision wasn't up to him. Helena had made good points, though negative, about all the other candidates, and it was hard to argue with her. And now, he had just asked for a day off, when he had just barely begun the job. Gerard likened himself as quite experienced in the management area, he figured Tom was probably looking for a new job or going to an interview. He would let it slide this time, but if it happened again, he intended to let Helena know.

∾

Helena emerged from her bedroom. It was noon. She pulled her nylon pink robe around her tightly and tied it closed. She sauntered into the kitchen and pulled the coffee filters from the cabinet. She filled the coffee carafe with water and poured it in the machine.

As the coffee brewed, she sat at her table and laid her head down. She wondered how she should plan her day. She was tired of having late nights haunted by the past and her thoughts. Or were her feelings what caused her such a burden? The smell of coffee began to fill the kitchen and she felt comforted by it. She slid out of her chair and leaned against the counter, staring at the machine. She stared as the liquid started to drain and the drips became less frequent, then she poured herself a cup. She added her cream and stirred. She opened the refrigerator and grabbed a loaf of bread to make some toast.

When she finished her breakfast, she wandered into the living room and turned on her stereo. The music always woke her up and gave her energy. She was still half-asleep, but she was waking up slowly but surely.

It was the weekend! What would she do? Shop? Call some friends? Catch up on reading her magazines? Go to the movies? She opened her French windows and sat on the ledge. She stared out at the neighborhood. It was a beautiful day. There was lots of sun and a light breeze. She felt a little sluggish and decided she would get dressed and go for a power walk.

She put on her running shoes and sweats and pulled up her hair in a ponytail. Then she bounded out the door and into the sunlight.

∾

Tom had received a letter from SMP Recruiting, Inc. It was the same message he had received in the e-mail from Blythe Walker. He still couldn't believe his luck. He couldn't wait to get started, but it didn't mean he didn't have his doubts. He hoped he could handle it. It was a high pressure industry and competitive, and it was his writing that would be at stake. Then again, maybe he was jumping the gun. He had yet to hear what the position entailed.

He had made reservations at a hotel in Sun Valley, about ten minutes away from the paper. One week of work at Advent and then he'd be on his way.

He checked his messages and received one from his sister, Rose. He had sent her an e-mail and she hadn't responded. He picked up the phone and dialed her number. She was living in New York.

"Hello?"

"Rose, it's Tom, sorry it took me so long to get back to you. How are you? Is everything alright?"

"Oh, yeah. Mom was worried about you."

"Yeah I know, I talked to her."

"That's good."

"So, what's up?"

"Nothing much."

"How's Billy?"

"Oh, we're not together anymore. That's kind of why I'm…well..not feeling too good."

"Aw, Rose, I'm sorry."

They talked a while longer, and Tom told her about his new possible job at the paper. She couldn't believe his luck either and gushed about how great it was. She said she wanted to visit him in California if he got the job. He said of course. He told her he'd try to come out and visit her, and then they hung up. He ran his hands through his hair and sat at the kitchen table. Rose had him worried, especially when it came to relationships. She had a history of jumping from one guy to another, as if looking for some kind of completion in whoever she was with. But as if he was one to talk. He wasn't much better at handling them either. She grew up stricken with a host of medical issues, and was depressed and often morose in her demeanor. He had reason to believe she was abusing painkillers. Everyone looked out for Rose. Rose was ill, Rose needs support, Rose is vulnerable. Shortly after their parents' divorce, she finally started seeing a therapist after she graduated from high school, because she was so withdrawn and angry. Tom blamed his parents for neglecting the signs and by the time they realized something was not right about her behavior, it was too late. Rose used to walk around the house with her headphones on and alienate everyone around her, even when they had company and around relatives. Sometimes their mother would tell her to stay in her room and then bring her dinner. Tom always thought she should encourage Rose to come out and socialize no matter how much she didn't want to and at least *talk* with her about it, but she didn't. She would let her simmer in her misery and made her seem like some pariah. Pretty soon, Rose made a name for herself as "the Strange One," and it only caused more embarrassment for their parents, not that they noticed anyway. When she moved to New York, she met Billy, a comic book artist. Tom was worried that she wouldn't be able to handle her life alone in the big city. She surprised him. She immediately landed a job at a bookstore and was able to afford a studio with Billy. Tom encouraged her to go to college, but she said she would rather wait for a while. Now that she was single again, Tom thought he should encourage her to apply. Their father, an architect, and their mother, a prosecutor, were furious when Rose ran out on college right after high school to move to New York, and they never let her forget it. They called her insistently, scolding her, and pushing her to apply. She ignored them and argued with them vehemently, no, she would not, she had no interest. Then they went to Tom, to try and get him to talk to her. He said he would try, and did, but to no avail.

"Rose will," he had assured his parents. "In due time. Just get off her back." He would have added, you are both to blame, but did not. He didn't want to get into it with them at the time.

As for her situation now that she was no longer with Billy, Tom just hoped that she kept the studio and remained employed.

∾

Helena returned from her walk feeling refreshed and rejuvenated. She decided she would order in Chinese and rent a movie that evening. She wanted to stay in, even though she had received an invitation to go out from a friend on her answering machine. She called back, and left a message that she wasn't feeling well. She was feeling fine, she just didn't feel like being around a lot of people. She sometimes found social situations draining, especially when she had to attend to so many meetings at work. Staying in by herself on the weekends was sometimes a welcome respite. She went out if she wanted to blow off some steam. But tonight was not one of those nights. Those kind of nights were becoming more and more infrequent, she realized, and wondered what was happening to her. Was she maturing? Were all the meditating and relaxation techniques paying off? Was she becoming a more balanced person? She felt intensely lonely less and less. She felt more and more comfortable just being alone.

Then her thoughts went to Shawn. What surprised her was how often she still thought about him. At that time, she believed that she wanted to get married someday, and he was near the top of the list. He didn't expect or demand things from her and that made her feel comfortable with him. She thought she loved him. She wasn't sure how he felt. When she began unknowingly expecting more from him, they began fighting. But he didn't want a commitment. She found it hard to believe. She thought he loved her. She was wrong.

They soon let go of each other. Now it all seemed to her like a dream where she only remembered bits and pieces. It was surreal and most of it didn't seem to make any sense.

Soon after, she began to forget the feeling of romance – the fun, the joy, the laughter, the sharing. The part that rings in the heart and says, "that's what I like, I like that he does that, there is no one in the world like him and he's mine." That's the best part: discovery, and feeling pleased by it.

Then comes the deep thinking things through, the question – what do I really want? It's either date casually, or commit. Dating casually is just a prelude to commitment, and when that doesn't happen, things fall apart. Committing too fast can be suffocating to both. If you're lucky, things can always be discussed. Things never worked out for her because she never got beyond her own personal demons. They seemed hot on her trail whichever option she chose, and she never seemed to shake them off. Still, trials and tribulations later, she played it safe with cynicism. She found herself not wanting to play anymore.

But Tom was changing all that. She felt something that she hadn't felt in a long time.

10

~

About 12 years ago, Helena had been accepted at a prestigious university to study for her MBA. She had just returned from Japan. Her father had accepted a temporary teaching position there and Helena and her mother had tagged along. Needless to say, the trip was terrible. Tensions were high between she and her parents and she felt like a real pain in the ass. She hardly even remembered the trip now, just bits and pieces.

She could lie to all her friends and say how fantastic it was, a great learning experience and all that, but the truth was: she was miserable.

Being from California, Helena had never felt the cold like she did in New York City. She arrived just before winter, at the tail-end of humidity season – August.

"You're going to love New York," her friend, Jennifer, had told her. "You'll love it in the summer when the heat cooks the garbage on the sidewalk and you can smell it from your apartment."

Helena supposed that Jennifer must know what she was talking about, since she used to model and spent a lot of time in New York at one time. Now, she was just her neighbor, slightly heavier and with a penchant for drinking and spontaneous sexual encounters with men.

Helena was with her mother, searching for an apartment. She had missed the deadline for accepting her assigned living quarters from the university, so they gave it away.

"You're going to love New York," her friend, Ruth, had told her. "There's a bar on every corner and you don't have to drive, and they're open all night."

They stayed at a youth hostel in the upper west side that was actually quite nice. They shared their room with two girls, one from England and the other from Russia. Helena was keeping a close eye on her suitcase. Besides having everything she would need until her boxes were shipped from California, it also contained a medium sized frosted glass bottle of citrus vodka, which she had stored neatly in a small, brown paper bag. It was a going away gift from her friend. She had been thinking about it almost every day, just waiting for a chance to get in there and have a drink. But she didn't want to drink it straight because she felt that was too "sloppy."

But she found that she was too busy to bother getting into the bottle. There were more important things to worry about, like finding a place for her to live and arranging for her things to be shipped from California.

Helena was cranky after having trudged four blocks looking at another apartment.

"How can you be so irresponsible! You better sign the paper, and send it right away! How could you not know!" her mother chastised her.

"Jesus, mom, if you say another goddamn word, I'm going to sock you!" Helena's anger was so intense, she really felt like she could throw a blow at her mother with no remorse.

Her mother stared at her with hardened eyes. They shuffled next to each other in silence for the next five blocks. The scenario was repeated the next day, and the next. Finally, after a visit to the university housing office, they found a household that needed one more roommate. It was $553.00 a month and was only two blocks away from campus.

"You should take that," her mother told her.

When they arrived at the apartment, a young Indian woman answered the door wearing a t-shirt and sweatpants. She was frantic and nervous.

"Hi! I'm so sorry, the place is a mess, I can show you around, can you hold on a second? I'll be right back!" She ran to her room and slammed the door.

The apartment was small, with a long, skinny hallway and a kitchen that looked like a hallway. The available room was the smallest one, with a small window, a view of the other building across the way and no sunlight. Helena was none too satisfied with any of the apartments she had seen, and felt like she was trapped in a mire of bad choices. She was angry at herself for not signing the paper over the summer guaranteeing her housing.

The living room was open and had a window leading out to a tiny balcony. There were lots of plants near the window and basic furnishings, a couch that didn't appear very comfortable, a dining table and coffee table, and a chair. No TV. The hardwood floors were dusty. Dishes were piled up high in the dark and musty kitchen.

Helena and her mother glanced around their surroundings cautiously and then footsteps came trumping down the hallway.

"Oh, by the way, I'm Sama," said the young Indian woman.

"I'm Helena."

"Hi! Okay, so this is the living room, those are Sylvia's plants, this is the kitchen. I'm sorry, it's such a mess -"

" - and Sylvia's room is down here, she's not here, she's on vacation, and my room is down the hall right here, and this would be your room. Well, if you decide to take it. Do you think you want it? Have you looked around at other places? It's a nice place, I mean, it's close to school and everything -"

"Yeah. I know. We've looked at some others, I'm not sure yet," Helena broke in, feeling tense from the quick pace of Sama's speech. She hesitated.

"Yeah, well, I think it's good, I mean, it's open you know, so I would jump on it, I mean, what school are you going to?"

"Business."

"Oh, yeah, okay, oh that's cool, well I hope you take it, I mean Sylvia's really nice and we're friends and we like to do things together."

"Oh."

"So, yeah, okay, well, I guess if you have any questions you can call me, here, let me get you my number." She ran off to her room and returned with a number scrawled on a torn piece of paper.

"Thanks."

They left the building and on the way down in the elevator, Helena's mother spoke.

"I think that's okay, Helena."

"I don't know."

"It's the best one, be reasonable," she said.

Helena didn't answer.

That night, Helena heard the sounds of people laughing outside her door. When on the roof earlier, sneaking a cigarette, many international youths had gathered, drinking out of green and dark amber bottles of beer, chatting and sitting at the tables, relaxed. She was reminded of college, when students wandered in and out of the dorm hallways with bottles in their hands and lazy smiles on their faces. It seemed like ages ago. She glanced at a young woman sitting near the doorway next to a young man, they looked relaxed and carefree, chatting easily while smoking cigarettes. Back in the room, Helena climbed to the top bunk and cuddled underneath the thin covers. She had no conception of what she was to do or where she would go. She felt suddenly lost and confused about what she was doing at this very time, why was she going to school again and where did she think it was going to take her. She shook off the feeling of fear and went back to acting as though she knew what she was doing. She slipped back into the persona of someone who was familiar with the city and the people, someone who could get along anywhere. She had long since identified herself as a sort of chameleon, conforming to whatever standard was kept wherever she found herself. She regarded this as a mature and outstanding trait, one that she had tried hard to cultivate. She expected others' acceptance and approval, but on the same token, if they didn't give it to her, she felt no remorse in striking them off her list and discounting them as any kind of potential acquaintance. She never stopped to think that people's disapproval of her was probably necessary, and was, in fact, inevitable. People moved in the world independent of each other, proud of the separation caused by their uniqueness.

The next morning, Helena and her mother had lunch and discussed her housing options. Helena felt irritated, but finally realized that it made the most sense to take the open room with Sama and Sylvia. She had not thought at all about what it would be like getting along with the two. Regardless, her feelings about them were a small matter in comparison to needing living quarters for the year. All other qualifications matched up, the location, the price and the general set-up: two young female roommates who were also students.

After securing the apartment, Helena knew it would be time for her mother to leave. She felt relief at the prospect. With her suitcase in tow, Helena made her way up to the apartment. Before leaving, they had gone shopping for a blanket, pillow and some groceries. Hauling her supplies up to the fourth floor, they entered the apartment and opened the heavy door. The super was with them and he set her up with keys and the contract. Helena's mother, in a last attempt to exert her influence, argued and snapped about the condition of the room.

"We need a new mattress."

"That's the only one we have."

"No no no. We need a new one."

"Okay, I'll try and find you one," said George, the super, a medium height African American man from Haiti.

Helena's mother pushed her way past him and grabbed her suitcase.

"Mom, I got it. Let go."

Helena looked at the super in embarrassment.

When Helena's mother left to throw out the kitchen garbage after cleaning as much of the apartment as she could, the super and Helena were left alone.

"Well, you have any problem, you know where I live, you just call, come over, whatever, ok? These girls, very nice girls, very nice. No problems."

"Yeah, okay," Helena answered.

Helena's mother returned and they proceeded to clean off the soiled mattress. After covering it with sheets, it wasn't so bad. Helena told herself she would just have to forget what lied underneath.

When classes started, she knew something was wrong. She was caught on account of tardiness and threatened expulsion. She gave her professor the excuse that she was homesick and on medication. But the problem was she was drinking heavily everyday and she couldn't stop. When she had a moment alone, she took out the bottle of vodka she had in her closet and unscrewed it. She took it into the kitchen and poured herself a glass straight over ice. The next day it happened all over again. Then the next. She stayed home and made one after another. She stayed in and only went out for food. She couldn't wake up for class, she couldn't follow lectures, and she could barely read. She finally confessed to her professor. He referred her to his wife who counseled her and recommended she see a professional counselor. She made an appointment. The counselor referred her to an outpatient rehab program offered through the school located in Mid-town.

Drinking was never a big deal. When she graduated from high school, her parents took her out to dinner and ordered two large bottles of beer. A congratulatory dinner deserved a little rule breaking. But they seemed so serious. They were sending her off to college, and they seemed apprehensive. It was her frailty. They didn't seem to trust her ability to make it on her own. Later, she realized they were just scared for her, and a little sad.

She should have seen the signs. Her career was flailing in L.A. even though an old mentor of hers had secured her a job at a well-known consulting firm. One month into it she felt excited and fresh. Three months into it, she felt something sorely lacking.

It was the day she came home for lunch with the intention of finding beer in the refrigerator. Two or three and she would be set to go back to work. The problem was – no beer. Helena panicked. How could she have miscalculated her supply? Was she becoming that dim? She became afraid to leave the house. She squished into a fetal position on the floor and called her doctor. No answer. She left a message that she was having a severe panic attack and COULD SHE PLEASE CALL ME BACK AS SOON AS HUMANLY POSSIBLE. She hung up. Oh God! She was starting to feel stomach cramps and she was shaking like a leaf. Then she had an idea – her next store neighbor.

She was in luck because Jennifer was home with her boyfriend, Ivan. They were sitting at her kitchen table with a six pack of beer in the middle of the table. Helena walked in casually. A few minutes into the greetings, she casually asked if she could have a beer. They offered enthusiastically. Thank God. She took it and sucked it down. She wanted another, but she felt that would be too forward. So the one would have to do, for now. They talked. She was in the right place. Jennifer was on her way to a job interview. Ivan was on his way to class. She was on the way to work.

At work, Helena was feeling satisfied and happy. But several hours later she became irritable. She felt the drink wearing off and now wanted another. But it wasn't possible. She'd have to wait until she got home.

She was starting to feel weird at work. It felt like everybody knew something that she didn't. She thought she might have a problem. She supposed that it's much more evident than the person with the problem likes to think. So she went on a campaign to stop. She had already signed up for meditation. She thought that cigarettes were the problem. She decided to go out less often. She would only last a few weeks at a time. She even called a hotline and stopped by an AA meeting, but she ran off as soon as she got to the door. No, not for her.

Admittedly, she was a mess. Shaken and confused, she visited the person she was supposed to see through the school's infirmary, and she was told to go to group therapy where there would be other students also suffering from alcohol or drug dependency. She accepted the directions, and made her first visit.

There were about ten other students there. All had different addictions. One guy, a law student, was addicted to cocaine. There was a petite, but vocal girl, who had been addicted to heroin. Three or four who never uttered a single word. Then Gabbie. A law student addicted to alcohol, like her. Then a Southern belle type, perky and always smiling, addicted to painkillers. It was like a bad B-movie.

Helena couldn't believe she had ended up where she was. She felt like a zombie. She wandered the streets of the city three times a week to the hospital, then to AA meetings nearly everyday.

School was a terrible experiment. She was so sick, she could hardly function. She was barely able to survive the cutthroat nature of business school. She stumbled into the building and she stumbled out, every day, lost, but trying to act "with it." She felt annihilated. Her dad convinced her not to leave, and didn't really believe how sick she was.

"You are recovering from a very serious illness," someone from one of her meetings told her.

Her dad thought differently. Her professor suggested that she defer, but that wasn't in the cards. She stayed and forced herself to do her best even as she stumbled out of class and into the hospital and into a meeting and back to class. It was nothing short of sheer hell. She had no time to be social, not to mention most functions held at school had a hefty amount of beer and alcohol, and she was not strong enough to be around it without breaking down and downing a few beers.

And a strange thing started happening. She began to get severely paranoid, convinced that others were talking about her at any given moment. On the street, in class, at restaurants and cafes. She even started to feel that others were trying to sabotage her. She would come home bewildered and emotional.

Her professors had noticed her odd behavior and one day, got her in a room and confronted her.

"You were late to the workshop the other day, and we had specifically asked everyone to be on time. What happened?" Professor Patel was tall and lean. He was a handsome man, with a youthful face and soft dark hair.

"I have other obligations to attend to," she replied.

"You've been absent, late. Oracle Inc. called me for a reference. I gave you a glowing review. I don't know if you'll be able to pull it off," he said.

They continued to hound her and the discussion escalated until Helena blurted out:

"I'm an alcoholic! I've gone into recovery."

They stared.

"OK, well," the two glanced at each other. They relaxed. "That's OK, you need to tell us these things, be open, communicate with us. If you don't tell us, we won't know what's going on."

They were serious, but irreverent at the same time. Helena realized that she had been alienating herself. They let her go, and Helena had felt a twinge of guilt, but was relieved that they were so understanding.

It wasn't the first time that personal issues had interfered with her school life.

In college, she was managing a small co-op that was on the verge of bankruptcy. It started one day when she couldn't get herself out of bed. She had managed to crawl her way to the bathroom and threw up in the toilet. Then she started crying and couldn't stop. She crawled back to her room and called her parents. She told them that she needed a break.

"You can't leave," her mother said.

"But I don't know what to do, mom."

"You'll be okay, just do your best."

Helena hung up and called her friend, Cara.

As soon as she answered, Helena was still crying.

"You have to ask for time off, Helena," said Cara. "You're having a nervous breakdown!"

"But I can't, I can't just leave."

Eventually, she did. She felt she had no choice. She was always the perfectionist, trying to do a million things at once – it was no surprise that this would have happened. She decided to take a semester off school and went to live in a house that her parents rented out. It was empty that year so she moved in. She tried to relax and recuperate. It helped, being away from everything. She still felt guilt about not being able to follow through, but some heavy sessions of therapy were helping her to find her way out of the confusion.

She traveled to visit friends in different cities, and felt like she was on overdrive. She took an internship at a financial group and managed to avert passes made to her from a supervisor. She got scared when she started to hallucinate at work. She returned home and crashed into a paralyzing depression. She floated out on a raft on the pool, going in circles and staring at the sky above. The hot sun burned her skin. She couldn't talk or sleep and felt like she had a sack of bricks on her shoulders. Her parents didn't seem to notice. They stared at her in silent repression.

When she returned to school, she felt refreshed. She managed to get a great deal on a house by the beach. It was in a small complex that was clean and had a well-manicured garden. An elderly couple usually rented out the one-bedroom apartments to people who came for the summer. The apartments were fully furnished. Nearly all who lived there in the fall were students, like her.

Then it happened. It was all too familiar. One day, as she was walking to the bus stop, she felt the darkness set in. It was a horrible feeling of despair and hopelessness. She knew the feeling well. It was an ugly way to greet the start of the semester. She made an appointment with the school psychiatrist and asked for an anti-depressant prescription. He gave her one. She had headaches for the first couple of weeks, but then it lifted. She started to feel normal.

It wasn't too long before she began to feel lonely, so she called a "friend," Joe, whom she had met when she was working at a record store the last semester. They had begun a passionate relationship and neither of them was sure whether it was really over yet. They started to see each other again, and Helena was happy to be able to share things with someone again. Then things with Joe started to fade. Helena was so steeped in her self-fulfillment that she couldn't understand what she was doing. That's when she called Shawn. He agreed to see her, but in typical Shawn fashion, denied all possibilities for a committed relationship. That was the beginning of the end.

Shawn had started getting methamphetamine for Helena. Helena had tried it some time ago when she had taken time off school. Her best friend Janie had given it to her at a party. It made her feel good. High and happy, like anything was possible. When she mentioned it to Shawn, he had presented it to her one day completely out of the blue. He shook the small plastic bag with white powder at her and said:

"I got a delivery from the speed fairy."

She got into it again, and began doing it every-day – when she woke up in the morning usually. It squelched the depression and got her through the year. To her surprise, she was able to stop as soon as she graduated, when her and Shawn broke up and she moved back home.

The final reunion between her and Shawn occurred when she was living in L.A. and sometime during her relationship with Byron. She had called him after breaking up with Lenny; she always felt somewhat comforted knowing he was still around. He was living in San Francisco. He returned her call and told her that he was "leery" because of what happened when they were together years ago. She couldn't blame him – she was not in a good state of mind. When he came out to visit her, she learned that he had not changed much and was still looking for a no strings attached relation-ship. They had gone out to dinner and then back to his friend's home for a while.

He walked her out to her car and then leaned in and began kissing her. They got in the back seat and kissed for a while.

"Do you want to go back to your place?" he asked.

"No."

He pulled back.

"Are you mad?" She asked.

"No." He paused. "I'm a little disappointed."

"I don't want to make you mad."

"No," he said. "I'm actually glad."

"You are? Why?"

"I'm just glad." He stretched his arms around her from behind and gave her a bear hug.

Then she made the mistake of asking him if he would be "with" her. He said no. She asked him what he was afraid of. He said he wasn't "afraid" of anything, he was just not into it. Then she became angry and got out of the car.

"God, Helena, I wish we could at least see each other and not have to end it storming off like this!"

"I just don't understand how you could say you love me and then not want to be with me...not want to be my boyfriend!"

"I try to understand you so I wish you could understand me, too."

She stopped for a second and thought about that. So he just wanted to be understood.

The truth was, it was her, too. She was pushing and he just pushed back. Neither of them had the capacity to understand each other. Compromise was not an option. She had been high and crazy for most of the last times she had been with him. Fighting became a regular event, and it was true that she became careless and haphazard, even borderline mean. Shawn was fundamentally cold, he didn't care much about anything, and was unsympathetic when Helena would try to confide in him. He was quiet and sullen, and had a way of looking down on her and dismissing her.

She thought about a line in the song, "I'd rather live in his world, than live without him in mine." She couldn't remember the title or the artist, but she remembered hearing it on the radio while she was driving somewhere, and she immediately thought of Shawn. She finally found out the name of the song: *Midnight Train to Georgia* by Gladys Knight and the Pips. She later realized that no one should have to live in anyone's world – especially when that person was a complete asshole.

They kept in touch after he left with phone calls. Then one night he had invited her to Thanksgiving dinner at his brother's house and she agreed to go. Then, at the last minute, she got cold feet and called and left a message telling him she couldn't make it. She felt a little guilty about it, but she was afraid of who might be there, possible family members, and she definitely didn't feel up to facing any of them. She even turned down an invitation to one of her best friend's wedding. She knew she wouldn't bode well.

They continued to call each other, about once a week. One night, he told her that he was feeling lonely. He said he had been with someone recently and it just "wasn't the same." Helena wasn't sure what he was implying. Then he said he wanted to get back together. She surprised herself when she said, no. She told him she didn't want to get hurt again.

"I don't want to get hurt again," she told him. "I'm sorry."

When he spoke again, he sounded sad. They had such a regrettable history together, to end it this way could be deemed as a sad occasion, but really, it was the best decision Helena had made in her life. Truthfully, she hated him.

They never spoke to each other again.

~

As she finished off her Chinese dinner, Helena wondered how things would work out with Tom. She wanted him to be happy with his life. If anything, she just wanted him to be satisfied with his work and reach his goals, just like she had in her life. If she had learned anything in her recovery, it was the idea of giving and how that returned good luck and fortune to her the more she gave. What comes around goes around.

She had straightened her life out, but she was always on edge. She knew that anything could happen at the drop of a hat. She remained prepared for what might happen in her life from now on. She had taken the action; it could only get better from here on out.

11

~

Tom went to work on Monday feeling stressed. He had only been there one month, and he was feeling pressure to go about his business as usual without giving away the fact that he didn't have to care as much since he might be leaving his job in two weeks. Pretending was always hard to do. He wasn't a good faker. Even as he walked in this morning, he felt Gerard eyeing him suspiciously. As Tom got situated in his cubicle, he saw Gerard making his way over to him. He stiffened and tried to look as busy as possible.

"So, Tom, how ya doin'?" he asked.

Tom looked up in surprise and smiled.

"Great! Excited about some new accounts I've got."

"If you need anything don't hesitate to call on me. I'm usually in my office or just walking around. Anyway, you have my cell number and my extension."

"Of course, of course, yes, I will."

Tom turned toward his computer and opened up a client database. Gerard was still there, leaning against his cubicle wall. Tom turned around and smiled again.

"Am I bothering ya?" asked Gerard.

"No, no. I'm just trying to get situated."

"OK, kid. Do you still need Friday off?"

"I do still need it off. My dad's surgery isn't going to change schedule just for me."

"Yeah. Where does your dad live?"

"Connecticut."

"Right, sorry to hear it. Angioplasty, huh?"

"Yep. We're all pretty worried. But, he's got good doctors, so... we're optimistic. Ever had anyone in your family get a heart attack?"

"Yeah, my grandfather had a couple. Eventually died of a stroke. It was terrible."

"Yeah, too bad. Sorry."

"It was a long time ago. Anyway, I'll leave you be now."

"Thanks. See you around Gerard."

"OK, Tom."

Tom waited until Gerard retreated to his office before breathing a sigh of relief. It was going to be a long week.

Before the end of his first day at work, the rain came pouring down outside. Most had not brought their umbrellas and everyone started complaining. Tom had made good progress on his first day. Securing two clients and getting four others' interest enough to send out information. Nonetheless, the day went by slowly, and Tom had to do everything he could to stay focused on his tasks at hand. Gerard had approached him again mid-day to ask about his progress. Tom hoped he wouldn't be this attentive all week long. He wouldn't be able to handle that.

At the end of the day, Tom stepped out of the office and into the rain. It was a long walk to his car. Soaked, he climbed in, started the engine and turned on the heater. He muttered to himself under his breath and wished he had a jacket. He used to find rain romantic, but now it was just bothersome, always pouncing on you last minute. He had definitely grown beyond his foolish "romantic period," which was somewhere in his first year of college, and then entered his cynical phase after Andrea had dumped him. He briefly entered a "doom and gloom" phase, where he didn't trust anybody. All his relationships were brief and detached emotionally. Now, he would say that he was in his "realism" period. He wouldn't say that he was ever a hedonist. Though he had good friends who were and he hung around them for many years after college, just after the time he graduated and before law school. But he never took them seriously. They knew how to have a good time. What he hated was that he had a habit of backtracking to his doom and gloom era, where he would withdraw and become very insecure.

He felt that this is what held him back from pursuing a career as an attorney. He didn't have the cocky self-assuredness that most attorneys seem to develop. His mother begged to differ, telling him that he would learn as he continued to practice in the field, that it was a process, learning how to be a good lawyer. But he despised the competition, and wanted to go into something he was passionate about, like writing.

He drove home, stopping by the grocery store on the way. The rain made the streetlights melt into red, yellow and green liquid shimmer as the windshield wipers swished back and forth, leaving trails of water on the window. Tom picked up ingredients for dinner, lettuce and avocado for a salad and frozen macaroni and cheese, canned soup and chili.

The grocer at the check out line, a thin woman with short, red-brown hair and pale green eyes, looked at him and smiled.

"Hi. Long day?"

"Yeah, kind of."

"Same here." She looked at him and smiled again.

"Well, for your sake, I hope you get off soon," he said.

"Yeah, thanks." She paused before giving him his receipt. "Actually, I get off in one hour."

He looked at her.

"Exactly?"

"Exactly one hour." She handed him his receipt. "Sign here please."

Tom's gaze lingered and he signed his receipt. She smiled again.

"OK, then." He smiled, picked up his bag and headed out the door.

Dinner was easy. Tom ripped apart the lettuce leaves and ran them under some water. He shook them dry, put them in a bowl and added some veggies. He drizzled some blue cheese dressing on it and crunched on it while the macaroni and cheese heated up in the microwave. He turned on his space heater in the living room. After dinner, he lied down on his couch and read the newspaper.

After a while he turned on the news to see the weather for the week. It was going to be a wet week, they predicted. This time, he would be prepared.

He looked at the clock and watched it turn to 6:55. Then he threw on his coat and went out the door. He arrived at the grocery store about 7:02. He saw the thin woman with red-brown hair and green eyes walk out of the store. He got out of the car, shut the door and leaned against it. She looked up and saw him. She smiled. He smiled back.

"Need a ride?" he asked.

"No, I've got my own car." She said coyly. "We checkers aren't that poor."

Tom laughed.

"Well, in that case, want to get a drink somewhere?"

She paused.

"Sure. How about if I meet you at Rudy's?"

∾

It was only three hours later, when the woman, Lucy, and Tom were kissing passionately on the doorstep of Tom's apartment. Tom, stopped and fumbled for his door key. They tripped into the apartment and Tom turned on a light. He didn't want it to be too bright. They continued kissing on the couch, while Tom slipped her out of her shirt. She had small breasts, and her body was thin as a rail. They made their way to the bedroom. There, Sam fumbled with Tom's belt and pulled off his pants.

This was just what he was looking for. A fling. He hoped she wasn't going to be expecting anything from him after this. Afterwards, Lucy got up and went to the bathroom. When she came back, she started to get dressed.

"Leaving so soon?" Tom asked.

"Not right away. Got anything to eat?"

Tom got out of bed and pulled on his pants.

"Right this way, darling."

Lucy sat at his kitchen table, while Tom blundered about in the kitchen looking for something to cook.

"How's chili? With beer?"

"That's fine."

Tom cooked up the canned chili, adding some spices to it. He came out with two bowls and set one in front of Lucy and the other across from her. Then he went back into the kitchen and got two beers from the refrigerator.

"Mmm. Not bad," Sam said, after a spoonful of chili.

"Thanks."

"So, what do you do, Mr. Overton?"

"Please, you can drop the formality. Call me Tom."

"Oh, yes, sorry Mr. President. Tom."

"I work in management consulting."

"Uh, huh. Interesting. And do you like it."

"It's OK. How long have you been at Hansen's Grocery?"

"Oh, for about a year now."

They spent the next few minutes eating in silence. Afterwards, Lucy got up and started looking around Tom's apartment. She examined a photo of a dog, his pet when he was a child, and an old picture of him and his family, taken at Christmas, also when he was a child.

"Well, I should really get home now."

"Really? Well, thanks. I mean. It was a good time."

"Yeah, thanks."

Then Tom thought fast and looked at her. Her eyes gave her away, and she quickly looked away and ran her fingers through her hair. Should he, or shouldn't he?

"Can I get your number?" He did.

"Yeah, sure."

He got her a piece of paper, and she jotted it down.

"Thanks, again," he said.

She looked at him, smiled and nodded.

She left the apartment and closed the door quietly. He heard her car start up from outside and speed off.

He cleared the bowls from the table, along with the bottles of beer. He sat on the couch and threw a blanket throw around his shoulders. It was freezing.

∽

"So you confirmed the interview? This Friday?"

"Yeah. He'll be here this Friday at 3 p.m."

Elise and Helena were at the day spa getting massages, something they treated themselves to on rare occasions.

"Three days, I can't wait."

"He sounded nice on the phone."

"Oh, I know he's nice. He's more than nice. I just *adore* him. There's nothing he could do that would disappoint me."

Helena couldn't see her, but Elise rolled her eyes. She could care less about this whole situation, but if it made Helena happy, she would oblige. She remembered what Helena had said at her birthday party not too long ago.

"Elise, be my best friend. You're really the best. I mean that."

Elise had smiled and took a sip of champagne.

"Anything for you."

The truth was, Elise secretly admired Helena, despite her tumultuous past. She was really an amazing person. She was perfect, but she didn't feel that she was. Anyone else could see it, but not her. She was too self-involved at times, that might have been her only flaw. Otherwise, she was perfect. She was strong, successful and beautiful. As an aside, Helena was also very generous, and she had the means by which to be. She seemed to have everything.

Elise sighed. They both sat up on their respective massage tables. Helena rubbed the crook of her neck.

"God, that felt good."

"You said it."

After their massages, they got dressed and made a trip to the cafeteria. They piled their trays high with salad from the salad bar and added an entrée. Organic whole wheat vegetable lasagna lay next to heaps of curried couscous and fried polenta. Steaming brown rice and tofu and broccoli shed their aromas from large silver deep dish pans. For dessert there was low-fat white chocolate yogurt and whipped mocha mousse. Elise and Helena had their fill and chatted about work in general, office gossip and things that irked them. They finished their meals, and said good bye in the parking lot.

∾

Tom woke up the next day ready to start another day at Advent. He dressed warmly and made sure to take his umbrella. Gerard made small talk, but by Thursday left him alone. Tom came home from work on Thursday and started packing for his trip to California. Then he suddenly thought about Lucy. He wondered if he should call her. He didn't want to be rude. So he got her number and picked up the phone.

"Hello."

"Hi, is this Lucy?"

"Yes."

"Hi, It's Tom, you know, from the grocery store."

"Oh, hi there. How's it going?"

"Pretty good. How are you?"

"Good, thanks."

There was a pause.

"I'm actually, going out of town tomorrow, or else I'd ask you to dinner."

"Really? I'd love to go. Thanks. Where are you going?"

"California. It's actually, for a job interview."

"Oh. So you might be moving?"

"Yeah. It's for a job at a newspaper."

"Oh, so you won't be consulting anymore."

"Well, hopefully, not."

"Well, that's great. I hope you get what you want. It's so important to like your job."

"I couldn't agree with you more. Have you ever been out west?"

"No, I was born and raised here."

"Local gal."

"Yep. Well, thanks for calling, maybe we can go out sometime when you get back. Give me a call. OK?"

"Sure."

They said their good byes and hung up. That wasn't so bad, thought Tom. She was really a nice girl. He was kind of sorry he might be leaving, otherwise, something could have transpired between him and Lucy. For now though, he had to focus on this interview. He was nervous. He tried to shake it off and repeat his mantras focusing on the power of positive thinking. There was a time when he fell into a mild slump that lasted about a year. It was after law school and he was in between jobs. He hadn't yet landed the job at the TV station. He felt as if he was going nowhere and was a failure. He tried his hand at a law firm and was so disappointed he quit and felt he had wasted his time in school. He was desperate. So he ended up buying some self-help tapes that taught visualization and meditation. They helped, and he went out and nabbed the job at the station.

He finished packing and laid out his ticket on the kitchen table. He ate dinner in front of the TV and went to bed early. Both excited and anxious, he tossed and turned for a good two hours. He tried to relax, only to fall asleep at one in the morning. His flight left at 8:50 a.m.

~

It happened to be an unusually slow day at the Herald. Elise Rudolph was enjoying the peace and quiet, and the fact that it was Friday. They had just finished their staff meeting and she was watching the clock waiting for this infamous Tom Overton to arrive at 3:30.

Tom arrived at the L.A. airport and flagged down a cab to his hotel, which was in the valley east of L.A. where the newspaper was located. It took a good hour and a half to get there. By the time he arrived, it was 2:00 p.m. He got dressed hurriedly and made his way down to the lobby. He waited for his cab. When it arrived he climbed in and gave the driver directions. He arrived at the Herald at 3:15 p.m. He opened the glass doors imprinted "Sun Valley Herald," and went to the front desk. A young woman with a headset was seated there and to her right were three women also wearing headsets at separate desks. An elderly gentleman was seated across from one of the women, placing an ad. Tom looked around and immediately felt tension in the air. He looked at the woman and approached her. She glanced at him, but didn't say anything.

"Hello. I have an appointment with an Elise Rudolph."

"OK, have a seat."

"Thank you."

He walked back to the entrance where he saw a row of seats and sat down. Another five minutes passed and he saw a curvy woman, about medium height, with blonde hair walking down the hallway leading to the front desk. She was wearing an emerald sateen shirt under a beige pants suit and high heels. He at first was awe struck by the authority with which she carried herself. She leaned in to the woman at the front desk and they whispered to each other, and then she glanced up at him and held up her finger to say "one moment." Then she opened a small doorway that reached up to their waists and called his name.

"Tom?"

He walked over to her and she reached out her hand.

"Elise. Nice to meet you."

"Thank you. Nice to meet you."

They walked down a hallway where there were framed photos of world events and, he presumed, local happenings. Images of war, destruction, disasters, happy children with ice cream on their faces, animals from the fair, fires.

"How was your flight?" Elise asked.

"Fine, thanks. Long."

They made their way into the newsroom, the quietness of which surprised Tom. He heard an occasional clacking of keyboards, but it immediately defused Tom's image of a newspaper. He thought there would be loud talking, rabid reporters following their editors around the newsroom, phones ringing. It was all that but much slower. Fluorescent lights lit up the room like a tanning booth. Tom had always hated fluorescent lighting. The news room was small, but cozy. He followed Elise into a small office, where he sat down across from her and she slid behind a desk.

"So let's see, you have some experience writing?"

"Yes. I brought some samples."

He took them out of his bag and gave them to her. Elise read them over.

"These aren't bad," she said.

"Thank you."

"Well, what we have open is our news clerk position. I hope you don't mind doing basic administrative work, if you do, then you probably wouldn't want to take this job. There's not much writing. The clerk handles the mail, the phones, and assists other reporters with some basic research. Every once in a while we might assign you a story. But you'll get to learn a lot, and many of our reporters and some copyeditors once were clerks."

Tom nodded.

"The pay is $15.00 an hour with full benefits, and it's a full-time position. Do you have any questions?"

"I think you answered most of them."

"OK, well, we'd like you to start as soon as you can. When do you think you can be here?"

"Well, I have to give my two-week notice – "

"I mean after that."

"Well, I have to drive from Chicago to here, so it will take me a few days."

"Oh, well that should be an adventure!"

"Yeah, it's going to take some planning. Hopefully, my car will hold up."

"Is this your first time in California?"

"No. I've been here before."

"It's a great place to live. Nothing beats the weather here in Southern cal."

"Yeah, that's what I've heard."

"Would you like a tour of the premises?"

"Sure."

"Follow me. You can leave your bag here."

He got up and waited for her to lead, and then they went back into the newsroom. Elise introduced him to some of the staffers at their desks, who were all friendly. She took him to the small library, the conference room, and the break room.

It was a short tour, but she talked a mile a minute, as if he were already on the job, and Tom found it a little annoying.

"And that ends it," Elise said as they returned to the small office.

"Great, thanks," Tom said. He picked up his bag and put it over his shoulder.

"So are you going to let me know officially whether you want the job? Or did I just ruin it for you?"

"No, I…do want it. I just need to find out how long it will take me to get here and all that."

"Great! I'm glad to have you here, really."

"Thanks, I appreciate this opportunity."

"You're welcome."

"Well, I guess I'll get going now. I'll let you know when I can be here. Is it okay if I call you?"

"Of course."

"Alright, I'll be in touch."

As soon as Tom left, Elise sat in her chair and leaned back. She looked at her watch. It was close to 4:30. She pulled up her basket on the computer and checked for the last few stories trickling in. She went over them and sent them through to the copy desk. Then she gathered up her things and left her office, turning off the lights and closing the door behind her.

On her way home, she held off on calling Helena. She didn't know why. She just didn't feel like calling her. It wasn't a game anymore. After their meeting today, she realized that this was a real person that they were dealing with, and she wanted to make sure he was a good clerk, if anything. She wanted to give him all the right tools to do his job, not keep him as some pawn just so Helena could pounce on him. It wasn't right.

Tom arrived at his hotel feeling uneasy. Was it really worth it? The pay was awfully low. Well, he could always work there for a year or so, and then if it didn't work out, he could just leave. He had options. Nothing was a done deal. He took a long, hot shower and crawled into bed. Now he would have to tell Advent and Gerard that he would be leaving. He knew they wouldn't be happy, but what could he do. He had to live his life.

Elise was opening her door when her phone rang. Helena. She picked it up.

"Hi, he came, he saw, he got hired."

"Oh! Elise, that's great! I am so excited! Thank you so much for doing this for me."

"Yeah, yeah, you're welcome."

"So when is he going to start?"

Elise gave her a rundown of the interview and said it would be a while. They chatted for another half hour before Elise told her she was really hungry and had to get some dinner. Helena obliged and let her go. As she hung up her phone, Helena realized that Tom would be offering his resignation soon and thought about calling Gerard to "check up" on things early next week. She would have to make sure not to sound too anxious, as if she knew something was up. Maybe she wouldn't call. Maybe she would. Maybe she would just wait for the call from Gerard. Whatever the case might be, she could hardly contain her excitement.

❧

Tom arrived in Chicago Saturday evening. He was tired and a bit stressed thinking about relocating and having to face Gerard on Monday. But he was also excited; he would be getting his foot in the door in the media world. He blasted off e-mails to his friends, his parents and Rose. He did some research finding an apartment in Sun Valley and booked a moving truck to take his larger furniture items and some boxes to California. He would drive his car with whatever he could stuff in the back and the trunk. He couldn't believe he was moving again so soon. Goodbye Chicago, hello California.

He wanted to celebrate. He picked up the phone and called Lucy. Then he hung up after the first ring. That might not be a good idea. Since he was leaving, it might be awkward getting together. Then again, she had told him to call her. He dialed again. Then he hung up. He went into his kitchen and popped a frozen spinach quiche into the microwave. He poured himself some red wine and ate alone. He sat for a while at the table and glanced at the paper's headlines. He finished off the last piece of his quiche and poured himself another glass of wine. He took a deep breath and held the paper with her number scrawled on it in his hand. He stood up, walked into the kitchen and threw it away in the garbage.

∽

Gerard Ripling was reviewing some files when Tom knocked on his door Monday afternoon.

"Yes?"

Tom opened the door wider and stared in cautiously.

"Hi, Gerard, you got a minute?"

"Sure, come on in." Gerard waved him in and motioned toward the chair across from his desk. "Sit down."

"Thanks."

"What's up?"

"Um, I'm not sure how to say this, but I'm offering my resignation. I got offered a job in California."

Gerard stared for a moment.

"You're leaving so soon? Is there something we can do for you?"

"No, the truth is I really want this other job, and I know you spent a lot of time with me and I thank you for that, but I'm afraid there's no talking me out of it."

"I see. Well, we'll have to just hire a new person. I'm disappointed. You were doing well. You have a lot of potential."

"Thank you. I appreciate everything you've done."

Gerard stared again. Tom glanced down and smiled nervously. Gerard didn't smile back.

"I'll have to let the others at the main office know then."

"Thanks, Gerard. It was great working with you."

"Thanks. We'll miss ya."

"Yeah."

"Well, have a good trip. When are you leaving?"

"Two weeks."

"Driving?"

"Yeah."

"OK, well, good luck Tom. I wish you the best."

"Thanks, Gerard. Take care."

Tom stood up and swiftly made his way out the door. His hands were clammy and he was starting to shake. He went to the restroom and took some deep breaths. He splashed some warm water on his face and straightened his tie. Then he left and went back to his cubicle. He glanced at his watch, he had one hour before the day was over.

The next two weeks were grueling, but Tom made the best out of it. Gerard was noticeably cold to him, but he remained friendly. He even gave

Tom a going away present on his last day, a box of cigars.

"He wasn't with us long, but he put in a hell of a performance. Tom, you will be missed and don't get too crazy over there in California. Drive safe and don't forget us," Gerard had said at a small going away party they had for Tom in the lunch room.

"It was a great experience working here at Advent, and I really appreciate everyone's support and guidance. If any of you are in California, I encourage you to give me a call," Tom said as others passed out cake. "Thanks a lot everybody."

∾

Helena got the call from Gerard on the Tuesday after Tom had given his notice.

"You're not gonna like this Helena."

"What?" she said innocently.

"We lost another one. Tom Overton just gave me his two weeks notice. He got a job in California. After one month with us!"

She paused. "Well, we've still got all those other applicants. We'll just have to pick the next best one."

"You're taking this well."

"I've accepted it. Sometimes we just have to deal with the turnover. Why don't we get a conference call together, you me and Kip and we'll pick another applicant. How's Thursday, 3 o' clock?"

"Sounds good."

"OK."

On Thursday, Gerard, Kip and Helena meticulously went over the resumes of the other applicants they had interviewed. The call lasted a good hour and they finally decided on an applicant. Helena was relieved to have gotten the new hire out of the way. She wondered how she should approach Tom. She thought about giving him a call at his desk. She was paralyzed with fear. She couldn't go through with it. What would she say?

"Hi, Tom, It's Helena. I hear you're moving out west. Where are you going to be working?" He would answer, the Sun Valley Herald. "Wow, really? My good friend is an editor there, Elise Rudolph?" "Yes, she's the one who hired me," he would say. "Well, what a coincidence. Listen, when you get into town, why don't we all go have lunch? Here's my number. Give me a call."

No. She couldn't do it. She would wait until he got situated first. But then she wouldn't know where to contact him. Unless, she showed up at the Herald unexpectedly and ran into him. She would say she was there visiting Elise. Yes, that sounded like a better plan. She called Elise and told her what she was thinking. Elise agreed to go along with it.

12

~

What many did not know, and what Helena had painstakingly hid from others, was something in her past that was jarringly disturbing, hurtful, painful, traumatic, a lost piece of her personal history that she only made peace with by filing it away as something unreal, something of a nightmare, that happened only in her sleep, where it was only discovered to be just that, a nightmare, an episode that would melt away upon awakening.

When Helena began to hear the voices, urgent and persistent, she began to lose touch with reality, and her behavior merged into the world of delusion, where her reality became confused with the circus of activity ripping through her mind. It's one thing to know that what one may be thinking could be faulty and false, and it would be in one's best interest to ignore it. But where Helena got into trouble was when she began acting on her thoughts. She believed she was getting messages from the television, and newspapers. She began reading the fine print in her junk mail, believing she was receiving messages from the government. She hoarded newspapers, one in particular, *The Los Angeles Times*. They laid in stacks on her futon frame in the living room, where she had transferred them from the trunk of her car, carting them in armfuls like a madwoman on the run. No one could take her papers, she needed them, they were important. She had dragged the futon mattress into her bedroom. When she had moved into this apartment, she had taken the second floor for its high ceiling. She had the plan to design it like a loft, with her bed in the living room corner, and the bedroom as a study for her computer and desk.

She felt as though her brain was on fire, literally, and her eyes vibrated behind her skull like electric balls of hardened jelly. They were telling her to flee, someone was after her, to hurt her, kill her. When she started talking about the mafia, it seemed all too real. She began to think that cars were following her, that certain people that she had passed in the streets were there on purpose, sent out by some transient government entity. There were messages in their clothing, giving symbolic commentary about her life, where she was and where she had been and where she was going. She began to read into car license plates, the jumble of nonsensical letter and numbers came to mean something to her, that they had been specifically designed to tell her about herself and people in her life.

Soon thereafter, things got worse. She was driving with her mother one day, when she believed the red truck in the parking lot was following her. She parked and followed the man as he exited from his vehicle. He went into the department store and she had been clutching her digital camera for a few days now, not letting it out of her sight. She followed the man into the Macy's men's department and began snapping his picture from behind. He was a large, bulky fellow, wearing a plaid shirt, jeans and cowboy boots. She continued to snap his picture, when he noticed her.

"What are you doing?!" he asked.

"Nothing." She whispered.

"Why do you keep taking my picture?"

She was silent. She began to get scared. Maybe she should just get out of there. When the man approached the sales person behind the counter, she began to panic.

"Can you talk to her? This girl is following me around taking my picture!"

The sales person stared at her, bewildered. She fled. Through the glass double doors and back out to the parking lot.

Her mother was waiting outside by the car. She was indifferent and unfazed. She was still, by the car, staring at her with quiet concern.

"OK. Let's go mom." Helena jumped back in the car behind the wheel as her mother got in next to her. She sped off and out of the parking lot.

It wasn't long after when all hell broke loose. It began as a series of events when Helena had kept forgetting her medication, and took a sales job that required a lot of travel. She was driving her broken down Honda Civic up and down the length of California, from L.A. to the Bay Area and back through the Central Valley. She found herself in a hotel room crying and not being able to stop. She was borderline hysterical, and the rain was coming down outside harder than ever. She had broken her toe and was wearing a slipper, getting soaked from head to toe in the rain as she traveled to and from her work site. She was driving all over Southern California, when she stopped at a gas station and drove away while the pump was still in her gas tank. The pump had been ripped off its seam, and as Helena drove away, bewildered, she was lucky it didn't cause an explosion. The reason Helena was so bewildered, was because she felt like her brain was on fire, and heard a circus of voices urgently commanding her to do things. When she arrived home, she believed that her father was out to kill her, and that the mafia was after her as well. Others seem to exist only to hurt her or betray her. She fled to the mall and began buying lingerie, for some non-existent fiance, of which she had announced her marriage to, to her parents and relatives. The problem was, when she had arranged a meeting for her and her parents to meet him, he did not show up at the restaurant. The reason for this was because he did not exist, but Helena was traveling between two worlds, what was going on in her mind, where no one could see or understand anything, and the outside world better known as, more or less, reality. But that was essentially the problem, what she believed was reality was in her head, and when she learned the contrary, that nothing she was thinking was real, she became terrified. She began arguing and getting angry. She started imaginary fights where she fought with these ghosts that flew out of her mind and into her apartment. She began throwing her water bottles around her apartment and picking up her dining room chairs and crashing them down on the table. She fled her apartment to meet her non-existent fiance at a hotel. When she arrived, he was nowhere to be found. Upon leaving she ran into a car when backing up, but fled the scene. Moments later, she called the police because she believed her father had killed her mother, and called 911 to investigate. She arrived at her parents' house and met the police. Her parents emerged from the house and were unharmed. She was subsequently arrested and taken away to the psychiatric emergency ward. What they had said to her was:

"You've caused a lot of trouble today, young lady."

Apparently, years later after the fact, her father informed her that her downstairs neighbors had heard the ruckus upstairs when she had been ransacking her apartment. They believed some kind of domestic violence was going on and called the police. The police arrived at the apartment, but she was not home. In a separate incident, the hotel matron had been informed by a guest that his car had been hit, and caught Helena's license plate as she was driving away. This hotel clerk had also called the police. Then Helena had called saying there was a murder going on at her parents' house. This was, clearly, the trouble she had caused.

Once in the psychiatric ward, they placed her in a room. She couldn't sit still. Moments later, for some unforeseen reason, they strapped her onto a gurney. The straps bit into her skin and she began yelling, asking them to release her. After about an hour, she was released and transferred to another hospital. There she remained for two months.

She met a girl who she had seen in the emergency ward. She was babbling about God and sin. She met her in the hospital. She was young, and always seemed to be wearing this yellow and black plaid shirt.

While in the hospital, she felt sensations and heard strange thoughts and commands, saw strange scenarios in her head, she just couldn't seem to clear her mind. They finally put her on a medication, apparently new, had had successful trials in Europe, and gave her a diagnosis. Running around the hospital, she hung around the lobby, where new patients would come and go. She would sit and wonder what was wrong with them and why they were there. One kid reminded her of her best friend from high school. All he did was go on and on about how his ex-girlfriend had screwed him over. She was scared when she saw two women on separate occasions with deep cuts and bandages all over their arms. Not that Helena was a stranger to cutting. She had been guilty of such many years ago, but would be terrified to actually have it so blatantly obvious. All she did was cover it up with a few bandages. Anyway, she had been drunk, alone, angry. It was the anger that drove her to such measures. Some had seen the bandages. No one really cared that much. She had ignored any effort to address the issue. She wanted to keep it to herself.

She tried to talk to some people. She couldn't even remember the conversations she had had immediately after she left. They had smoke breaks once a day. Sometimes Helena would ask to have a cigarette, even though they weren't her's, and it was somewhat of an imposition on the nurse. She wasn't sure, how that system worked, if a patient somehow had his/her cigarettes confiscated, or if their family members had bought them for them. When she asked to have a cigarette, somehow she had the feeling that she was taking from someone else's pack. But the nurse would sometimes give one to her, other times, Helena was somehow scared to ask and so went without one.

They had transferred her to another floor about a month into her stay. She had only found out later that she had gotten out of being transferred to a state facility under state conservatorship because at her hearing, which her parents had attended with her, her father knew the judge, and apparently, she had done him a favor, and left her under her parents' care. Her father had been able to secure her another month in the private hospital. (That's what happens, when you have a father in high places.) It was a nice hospital, actually, clean, of course, and she slept in her bed and ate her square three meals a day in the cafeteria. She participated in arts and crafts, and basketball in the gym. The social workers were nice to her, and they would smile and call her by her name.

When she was finally released, she transitioned into a rehabilitation center located downtown. It was an old hotel that was renovated into a rehabilitation facility. She had a room that she shared with a roommate, then later was transferred to a room to herself. She had a couple of roommates, one of them was an older lady who always cuddled with a large white fluffy stuffed animal, a bear or a cat, she couldn't remember quite which. When she left she gave Helena a stuffed cat made from brown and orange quilt covering with buttons for eyes. Helena accepted the cat, which she still has in her bedroom and her parents' home. She learned about keeping mementos that would remind one of certain times and events in one's life, even if they were not very pleasant. A friend had told her that it would remind her of what not to do. She said it in reference to a necklace that a guy had given her which she still wore every once in a while. It was gold with "I love you" engrained along the chain. "What happened?" Helena had asked. She paused before saying, "I was date raped." When she had told her this, Helena had been stunned. Her first instinct would be to throw everything out, burn old letters and get rid of any remnants of that person. Actually, she kept old letters, to remind her of what had happened, and in a sense, keep her from making the same mistakes. She needed to remember the course of events, the feelings, in order to process and heal. Getting rid of all memories, was akin to denial, and would only keep you in pain.

The meals at the rehab center were better than the ones in the hospital. She liked the dining area, a group of round tables gathered together next to a kind of living room area, where there was a couch and TV. It reminded her more of a home, not like the sterility of a hospital cafeteria. In the hospital, patients were rounded up and made to wait in line, behind the locked doors, to be escorted single file to the cafeteria. The rehab facility was more open, letting consumers come and go as they pleased. The only restriction she didn't like was that all consumers were made to wake up in the morning, for breakfast, and their room doors were subsequently locked, so they were forced to wander the grounds and only go back to their rooms later in the afternoon. Helena would get so sleepy after breakfast, (they also did not serve coffee), she sometimes would fall asleep on the couch, only to be woken up and told she could not sleep.

She had kitchen duty once a week, where she cleaned up the tables, and washed the dishes. She liked mealtimes, because other consumers would say Hi, and were friendly. She befriended a young man, Terence, who she came to talk to and hang around with. He must have thought she was young like him, she had the image of a young twenty-something, where in actuality she was in her thirties. But she hung around him anyway. He was always drinking instant coffee that he bought when they went on their daily afternoon trip to the liquor store across the street, where they could buy snacks. He would buy instant coffee and mix it in a cup of tap water from his bathroom. He smoked constantly. He had also shaved his eyebrows and had no eyelashes. He was tall, with sandy hair and blue eyes. All Helena knew, was that she was somewhat lonely, and he was attractive. It felt nice to have a kind of friend. They had been reprimanded by the staff for embracing. Each of them had said they would stop, and they had later laughed about it.

Despite the reprimand, Helena liked the staff. They were for the most part very nice, and she liked the idea that others were there to kind of care for her.

Nonetheless, Helena was eager to leave. In an appointment with her counselor, she was able to negotiate an earlier leave date. They wanted to keep her another few weeks or so, but they let her forgo that date. Hence, she was finally released, and allowed to go home.

When she arrived home, she felt uneasy. Her things had all been moved into her old bedroom, and it was clean and organized. The last time she had been in the world, so to speak, she had been in her old apartment, where it was slightly messy and lonely. Now she was home again, and it only took a short while before she felt comforted under her parents' care, in the house she grew up in.

For the next few years, Helena had puttered around the house, watched TV and slept in, while sedated from medication. Her fate made a daring turn when she began to attend support groups for recovery from a diagnosed mental illness, and made friends. She grew stronger, and began look-ing for work related to her degree in business. She finally landed the job at Advent, and moved to Los Angeles. It was a struggle and a risk to make her way out of the hole she had been in, and back into the land of the living. She felt she had been relegated to another planet, and then decided to make her way back to earth.

To her relief, earth was halfway liveable. Judging from her bank account, and her promotion, she had added up a series of successes, and was proud of it.

All that was left, was love.

13

~

Tom's first day at the paper was hectic. Everyone moved fast, but he had to remind himself that he had certain responsibilities and to remain focused on those instead of worrying about what others were doing. He gathered his paperwork, sifted through the mail and transferred calls. At the end of the day, things started to slow down. Elise called him into her office. Tom entered and sat down.

"How's it going?" she asked.

"Good."

"Do you have any questions?"

"No, not right now."

"OK, well, I called you in because I want to explain to you more about the paper and how we work, so I'd like to take you out to lunch tomorrow. Do you have time?"

Tom paused.

"Sure, yeah, I'd like to learn more about what you do here."

"Great. Let's say 12:30 tomorrow."

"OK, great."

Tom left Elise's office and returned to his desk. Was it him, or was she coming on to him? He felt some vague trace of flirtation. She was very dominating. No, everybody was basically very friendly and close, so she probably just wanted to let him in on the loop. Still, something about her rubbed him the wrong way. But she was his boss, so he would have to go along with her. He didn't want to disappoint her in any way. One thing was for sure, they were a lot less nurturing here than at Advent. Having Elise pay special attention to him was something he thought he should take advantage of.

∽

As the days went by, Elise warded off Helena's evening calls. She had to admit, she was in love with Tom. She didn't want to set things up for Helena anymore. She was dazzled by him and she didn't feel that she had to give an excuse as to why. She didn't feel she had to justify it to anyone. Working so close to him was too much for her to handle. She wanted him to be with her, not Helena, not anyone else. She felt it from the first day, but she couldn't admit it to herself then. She knew she felt an attraction to him, but she subconsciously fought it off. Now, she could no longer deny it. She was falling for him.

Had Helena gone with her first plan to call Tom and set up a lunch date before he left Advent, she might have been able to intercept him from Elise. But she had relied on Elise once again to participate in her game plan. Now, even on the rare occasion that Elise did talk to Helena, Elise insisted that she was too busy that week or that day to get the ball with Helena and Tom rolling.

Helena became more anxious by the day. Finally, she decided she would drop in at the Herald unannounced. She wore her best outfit, did her hair and make-up and spritzed on her favorite perfume. When she arrived, Tom was nowhere to be seen. She saw Elise, who had to do everything from panicking when she saw her.

"What are you doing here Helena?"

"I thought we could make our lunch plans today, remember?"

"Tom's out on an errand."

"When is he coming back?"

"I don't know. Listen, Helena, we'll make the date. How's tomorrow?"

"But he's supposed to run into me, remember, the plan?" Helena was starting to feel foolish. Things weren't turning out the way they were supposed to. "I'll wait until he gets here."

Elise couldn't stop her. OK, so they would go ahead with the plan. It didn't mean it would stop her from getting Tom. She was already ahead of Helena. She worked with him everyday. She saw him everyday. She had more chances to prove she was the girl for him. She already felt he was looking at her in a different way – a way that went beyond mere boss and employee relations. That was her prerogative, to slowly seduce him to the point where he would be irresistibly attracted to her. She had done it before, and she could do it again. Tom was no different.

Their lunch together had cemented Elise's feelings for him. He was easygoing, but tenacious, and had a dry sense of humor. She felt he had a mysterious side that made him somewhat unattainable, an independence that was enigmatic. All these qualities fascinated her, and like a vampire, she wanted more.

Lucky for her, Tom called in and Elise was able to give him another errand so he wouldn't be back for a while. She told Helena, who looked defeated. She decided to go home, while Elise told her she would arrange for the lunch soon. She told Helena to call the newspaper and talk to Tom, telling him that she found out where he was from the managers in Chicago. Then she could tell him she knew Elise and they could all go to lunch together. Helena agreed with this option, and left.

On the way home, Helena picked up dinner. She was starting to feel depressed. Tomorrow was Friday, and she decided she should call Tom and get it over with as soon as possible. She was nervous, but she reminded herself how far she'd come to nab him, and told herself she couldn't stop now.

Elise was breathing a sigh of relief after Helena had left. She would have to confess to Tom how she felt. She would arrange for some of the staffers to go for drinks after work and invite Tom, then she could make her move. Tomorrow would be a good day since it was Friday. She emailed some of the staffers and received an enthusiastic response in return. She received Tom's response later than the others, which made her nervous thinking that he was going to decline the invitation. She finally received it later in the evening, and, to her delight, he had accepted the invite. They were all to meet at a local bar right after work.

∾

Tom was surprised the next day at work to receive a call from Helena Park.

"Hello, Tom? This is Helena Park from Advent Solutions."

"Hi, Helena, how have you been. Listen, I'm really sorry to have run out on you so early. I – "

"No, that's okay."

"Is there something I can do for you?"

"Well, I'm calling because I happen to have a good friend who works with you. Elise Rudolph?"

"Oh, you know Elise?"

"Yes, and I was so surprised to hear you had transferred, I just had to call and say hello."

"Wow, what a coincidence."

"Anyway, I was wondering if you'd like to join Elise and I for lunch sometime. She tells me you're doing really well and they are very glad to have hired you."

"Thank you. I'm enjoying it. As for lunch, sure, that would be great."

"How's tomorrow at noon? There's this great brunch place called Freddy's and it's near the paper. I can give you directions."

Tom jotted down the directions.

"Sure, sounds good. I'll see you both there."

When Tom hung up, he immediately became nervous. He never thought he would see Helena again. It wasn't like he had a crush on her or anything, he just felt something when he was with her. At the same time, he had to admit that he was kind of falling for Elise, his boss. They had lunch together quite a few times, and he was impressed by her knowledge of the newspaper business and current events. He liked that. It was kind of a turn-on. Helena was very attractive, but Elise had a unique look. Helena was petite, while Elise was curvy, but not overweight. Helena a darker look, and Elise a blonde, lighter look.

The end of the day was approaching, and Tom remembered he had to meet everyone at the restaurant. He finished up his to-do's and turned off his computer. Then he threw on his jacket and left.

∾

Tom opened the door of the bar and quickly made his way toward the restaurant side, where he spotted Elise and some of the other Herald staffers seated at a large table.

"Hi, Tom!" they all greeted him enthusiastically.

He sat down and took hold of a menu. Everyone talked over live music from the stage, which filtered into the restaurant side as the waitress came around and asked if anyone wanted to start with a drink. They all ordered their favorites, some peered at the drink menu to experiment. In all there were ten people at the table. Tom ordered a calamari dish and a beer. Elise sat next to him and smiled.

"I'm glad you came!"

"Yeah. I'm starving."

They all engaged in playful banter and continued when the food arrived.

"So how're you liking the new job, Tom?" a staffer, Tim, asked him.

"It's good, I like it."

"We're not getting on your nerves yet?"

"Nah, it's cool."

"Talk to me again after three months," he laughed.

"Shut up Tim, don't get him paranoid!" Elise said.

"That's OK, I'm already paranoid," Tom said.

"Really, why?" Elise asked.

"It's part of my nature."

"Well, that can't be good," said Sheila, another staffer.

Tom didn't answer. He shrugged and took a sip of his beer.

"We won't add to your insecurities," Elise said.

"Yeah right," Sheila retorted.

After dinner, they ordered another round of drinks and some staffers went to hang around the bar. Tom had about five beers and a couple of cocktails. He was starting to feel drunk. He looked at Elise and leaned into her face as they sat together, while others came and went. He wanted to kiss her, but maintained control. Elise had her third drink and stopped. She didn't want to get too drunk with Tom for fear she might do something foolish. She had to remain sober enough for "the talk."

Time ticked by, and before they knew it, it was nearing midnight. Some of the staffers were beginning to leave, said their good byes and gathered their belongings together. Elise and a drunk Tom were the last to trickle out. Once outside, Elise asked Tom how he was doing.

"I'm great!" He began laughing.

Elise's plan was cut short when she turned her face to meet him, and found Tom's hands wrapped around her face. He drew her to him and gave her a long, deep, but not sloppy, kiss.

She was stunned. Now what? She had gotten what she wanted. But not in the way she had planned. She looked at him and, instinctually, wrapped her hands around his head and drew him to her and kissed him back.

Tom smiled.

"Now, I feel even better."

Elise sighed and smiled.

"Tom, I have to say –"

"You want to keep this quiet, right?"

"Well, yeah. It's really important that we keep this quiet."

"OK. No problem."

They disentangled themselves from each other and sat on a bench outside the restaurant. Elise took out a cigarette and lit it. Tom reached out to her with his hand.

"May I?"

"Of course."

"He inhaled and handed it back to her. He made rings with the smoke.

"Isn't smoke just beautiful? The way it curls and twists in the night air."

They sat, quietly, not knowing what to say. Elise was just tipsy enough to not care about what just happened. Her cell phone rang. She took it out and looked at the screen. It was Helena. She let it ring and didn't answer.

"Aren't you going to get that? Could be important, could be an emergency..." Tom murmured.

"No, I'll check my messages later." She paused. "Tom, I like you."

"What's that?"

Elise realized she was talking low.

"I said, I like you."

"Uh-huh. What? You do?"

"Yes, how do you feel about me?"

"I like you, too, Elise."

"Where do we go from here?"

"I don't know."

Tom looked at her.

"I think it's time I went home now, Elise," he said.

"OK."

Tom got up and looked around. He saw a gas station across the street and began walking toward it.

"Where are you going?" Asked Elise.

"Coffee, Elise. I need some coffee."

He sauntered casually toward the gas station, and Elise watched his retreating form. He strode with a sort of dignified carelessness. She looked down and stubbed her cigarette out on the ground with her shoe. Then she walked to her car and drove home.

∾

The next morning, Tom woke up and almost forgot he was supposed to meet Helena and Elise for brunch. It was only when he got into the shower that he remembered what had happened the night before. Water dripped over his dark hair and ran down his face as he stood there, wondering how he could have got involved with his higher up. But he was drunk. So was she. Or so he thought. He could hardly remember the conversation, but he remembered enough.

When he arrived at Freddy's, Helena was already there, but Elise had not arrived yet.

"Hello, Helena." She rose from her seat and gave him a hug.

"Hello, Tom. It's so nice to see you. Elise should be here any minute."

Tom sat down and stared at Helena. They locked eyes, and Helena began to fall into those deep wells, but she broke the gaze and began to study her menu.

"You know what's great here are the eggs Benedict. They also have a fabulous shrimp omelet with Spanish sauce."

At that moment, Elise strode in the door and came toward them.

"Hi!" She looked at Tom briefly and tried not to think about the night before. She hugged them both and sat down.

"Isn't it just something else that Helena and I happen to be friends?"

"When I heard you were at the Sun Valley Herald, I just couldn't believe it!" said Helena.

"Thanks for inviting me to brunch, it's nice to have friends around here," said Tom.

"How are you liking L.A.?" Helena asked.

"It's nice. I like it," he answered.

Helena suddenly found herself at a loss for words. Something strange was going on. She felt tension in the air. Tell him you are available as a tour guide, she told herself. Do it, just do it! She was speechless. She stared down at her menu, when Elise broke the silence.

"Have either of you seen that movie "Rapture?" It's supposed to be really amazing."

Helena looked up and Tom shot a glance at her. They both shook their heads, no. The waitress approached the table and they ordered. Helena gulped her coffee and remained silent. Elise looked at her briefly with wide eyes and tried to lightly kick her under the table. Helena responded by wiping her mouth and excusing herself. She got up and went toward the restroom. Elise waited until she was out of sight and then turned to Tom.

"Listen, Tom, don't mention anything to Helena, okay?"

"Yeah, okay. Oh, I wanted to ask you – would you like to come by my place later tonight? I can make you dinner."

"No, I can't. I made plans."

Helena made her way out of the restroom. She sat back down and smiled nervously. Finally, she spoke.

"So, how do you like your new job?"

Tom, distracted by Elise, answered hastily.

"It's great. I'm enjoying it. Elise is great to work with. We have a good time, right, Elise?"

"Sure," she said, relieved that Helena had finally said something, but unnerved by Tom's behavior. This time she excused herself and went to the restroom. She didn't have to worry about leaving them alone, it was clear that Tom had fallen for her. Now she was really in trouble. She reached in her purse for some pills. She had forgotten them. Damn, she thought.

When she returned to the table, the food had arrived. She flagged down the waitress and ordered some champagne. Tom asked for a glass as well, while Helena declined.

While Elise had been away, Tom and Helena had remained silent. Helena had finally asked one question and Tom, in rote fashion, had answered.

"So, what did you order?"

"The vegetable omelet."

They all began eating and Elise and Tom began talking about work, while Helena found herself trying to follow their stories. Tom had not asked her about Advent nor did he seem to demonstrate any interest in her at all. She didn't know what to do.

She wanted to go in the bathroom and cry, but she straightened herself up and chatted and laughed with them. She felt like an outsider, a third wheel. They finished their meals and Elise and Tom were clearly tipsy from the champagne. Not a surprise with Elise, thought Helena.

"Well, that was about one of the best brunches I've had. This place is awesome," Tom said.

They all stood up after paying the bill and made their way out of the restaurant.

"It was great seeing you Helena. I hope to see you again," Tom turned to her and gave her a hug.

"Same here, she said, now that we both live here, that won't be a problem."

"Right." There was another silence as they stared at each other and looked away.

"Let's do this again," Tom finally said.

"OK," Helena agreed. Then they walked their separate ways.

Helena got in her car and started the engine, as she drove away, she adjusted the rearview mirror and glanced in it. There right in front of her eyes, she saw Elise and Tom kissing and hugging in the parking lot of Freddy's. She screeched on the brakes and caused a car in back of her to honk. Was that a friendly kiss? It didn't matter, there was no such thing as a friendly kiss on the mouth, not from what she saw. That wasn't friendly. She pulled over sharply to the curb and stared at the steering wheel. She was so angry she didn't know what to do. She began crying. How could Elise betray her like that? After everything that had happened, she turns around and does this? She put her hands over her face and began bawling loudly. She was destined for failure. She had choked at brunch and now Elise had him.

When she got home, she sat down at her breakfast nook and stared into space. She pondered what she should do. If she let things go on like this, she would never forgive herself. If she confronted Elise, she would have to devise a game plan. But she realized that she was forgetting the most important thing – Tom. She would have to come clean about everything to him, it was the only way to resolve the situation and come away with a clean conscience.

Elise had not known that Helena had seen her and Tom in the parking lot. She went home that day and managed to avoid Tom's invitations to dinner, at least for that night. She was sure that she had to tell him about Helena and confess that being with him wasn't right, even though that was what she wanted. She felt so conflicted she didn't know which way to turn. She didn't know what was more important – her loyalty to her best friend, or her romance with her best friend's crush. Her attraction to him had been irresistible, she couldn't control how she felt. At the same time, she should have known she was working on Helena's behalf and checked out her feelings at the door.

Tom was confused about Elise's refusal to have dinner with him. He noticed there was something holding her back. He called her the next day, but got her voicemail and left a short message asking her to call him back. As the day wore on into the evening, he didn't hear from her. He didn't want to call her again, for fear of looking desperate, but he wanted to just hear her voice. Then the phone rang. He answered it quickly.

"Hello, Tom?"

"Yes?"

"This is Helena."

"Helena? Hi…"

"Hi, listen, I know you might be surprised to hear from me, but I need to talk to you."

"Really? Okay, about what?"

"Well, I would like to see you in person. Do you think I could come over to your place, or – "

"No," Tom was afraid to show her his unkempt quarters. "Do you want to meet somewhere?"

"Can you come to my place?"

"Sure."

Helena gave him directions to her place and Tom wrote them down.

"OK, I'll leave in about ten minutes," he said.

"Alright, I'll see you soon."

"Helena."

"Yes?"

"Are you okay?"

She paused.

"Just get here soon," she said, and hung up the phone.

~

Tom threw his sweatpants in the laundry basket and pulled on a pair of jeans. Shirtless, he looked at himself in his full-length mirror and tousled his hair. He went to his closet and looked through his shirts. He pulled out a chocolate brown flannel button down and threw it over his shoulders and slipped his arms through the sleeves. He grabbed his keys and was out the door.

On the way to Helena's, he stopped by the grocery store and picked up a cooked rotisserie chicken and two pre-made salads.

The freeway was packed with weekend traffic. Tom opened his windows and whistled as the night air blew in his face. He was looking forward to seeing Helena, but he was a little uneasy about the phone call and what exactly she had to see him for. She sounded just a notch above distraught, he wondered why she would call him above all. Was she pregnant and needed a man's opinion/advice? Was she sick? Cancer? He continued to speculate, and had no idea. He held in his hand the directions to her home, and followed them carefully. She lived about a half hour away, she had told him on the phone. He reached her neighborhood, which was very nice. He slowed down and inspected the addresses until he finally found it. He pulled up and parked at the curb. The house was painted sky blue and cream and the front porch light was on. Tom got out of the car and opened the back seat for the chicken and salads. He locked the doors of his Dodge SUV and made his way to the front door.

Helena had been nervously straightening up her home and looking in the mirror every ten minutes. When the doorbell rang, she immediately wanted to call off the whole thing and not answer the door. She couldn't, it was too late. Too late for everything, she thought. She had spun a scheme and it had gone awry. But she wasn't about to let Elise get the best of her. She would get to Tom first; that bitch had another thing coming.

Helena answered the door with a humble smile.

"Hi, Tom. Thanks for coming."

"Sure."

He walked in and followed Helena to the living room.

"You've got a beautiful place here," he said.

"Thank you."

"I brought some dinner. I hope you like chicken."

"I have no problem with chicken. Thank you, that was thoughtful of you."

Tom followed her into the kitchen and set the grocery bag on the counter. He pulled out the chicken and salad. Helena fished out two plates and silverware, along with two glasses of water.

"Sorry, I don't drink," Helena said.

"I guess it's good I skipped the wine then."

They ate together in silence for the first few minutes.

"This is delicious."

"It's organic." Tom paused.

"So, how are things at Advent?"

"Good. Busy."

"I know you travel a lot, that must really take a toll on you."

"It does, sometimes, but I got used to it. Pretty soon you get to know that a three-hour time difference means an excuse to put off a load of work for a few days."

Tom smirked.

Helena looked at him and took a sip of her water.

"You don't have to do much traveling at the Herald."

"No, it's all on-site. Except when I have to go out on an errand."

"Do you like that? Not having to travel?"

"Not necessarily, I could use a good plane ride every now and then. I do find it a bit draining though."

"How was your drive from Illinois to here?"

"It was fun."

Helena was enjoying her conversation with Tom, she almost thought to skip having to tell him the real reason she asked to see him. She was having a good time with him and she didn't want to ruin it. He would surely be a little upset. She wondered if he would bring it up. Maybe he wouldn't. Then she thought of Elise. She decided to bite the bullet.

"Tom, there's something I have to tell you."

"Are you in trouble, Helena?"

"No, I'm not in trouble. I have something to confess. About your job at the Herald. I set that up. I set it up so that you would be closer to me in California. Elise was in on it, too."

Tom furrowed his brows and looked at her in disbelief.

"I know about you and Elise, Tom. I saw you two in the parking lot at Freddy's yesterday! That's why I'm telling you all about what we did, because it wasn't supposed to turn out that way! Elise...she betrayed me. She went after you."

"You set me up? All this was a lie?"

"Not a lie. I just wanted to help." She paused. Then she said it. She had nothing to lose.

"I think I'm in love with you."

"No, it was a lie, Helena. You – how could you, what were you thinking? I mean, I don't know what to say."

"I'm sorry, Tom."

Tom was quiet. Helena continued.

"I got you a job at the newspaper, because I wanted you to write and get a career off the ground."

Tom stared at her.

"I think I'm in love with Elise."

Helena felt her face getting hot.

"What?"

"I said, I think I might be in love with Elise."

"How the hell did that happen?"

"It happened."

"She's my best friend."

Tom stood up and made his way to the door. He opened it and walked outside. Helena ran after him and began crying.

"I hate you! After everything I did for you and you fall for my best friend! How could you! What kind of person are you?"

"Helena, how was I supposed to know that you were concocting this grand scheme behind my back? Were you ever going to tell me about it, if you hadn't seen Elise and I together? Would you have made me believe I actually got this job from my own merit and gone along with the plan forever?"

"I would have told you eventually."

"I'm not sure I can believe you."

"Are you really in love with her?"

"I don't know. Maybe."

"Oh, shit." Helena sat down on the front porch steps and started sobbing. "I trusted her. How could she do this to me?"

"What do you mean?"

"I mean, she was in on it too. She knew from Day One that I wanted you, and she helped me. We planned it together. She knew the headhunter and she got rid of the person on staff to make room for you and she did the mock interview and hired you. She did it for me. She wasn't supposed to fall for you."

"Oh. Partners in crime. Isn't that just lovely."

"Let me ask you a question," Helena said. "Do you like your job?"

"Yeah, I like it."

"Then why don't you just keep it. Forget about me, forget about Elise. Just do your job."

"Well, okay, but that doesn't really make things all better."

"You have to make a decision, Tom. Me or her."

Tom looked at her face. It was sad. The moonlight made her skin almost translucent, like a fairy floating in the skies with wings. He remembered how he had liked her from the beginning, how he reminded her of Andrea. He continued to stare at her. This time neither one of them looked away. Helena fell into his eyes. They were the same, deep wells that went to the core of his soul, sharp blue meteor bombs. She continued to fall and then they burst and she covered her face with her hands and started to sob. Tom took her in his arms and held her. They stayed together that night in Helena's house. He led her to her bedroom and laid her down on her bed. He lay down next to her and stroked her hair until she fell asleep.

The next morning, Tom got up early and went into the kitchen. He looked around her home and noted how clean and neat everything was. Her art was perfectly framed and placed strategically around the house, serving its purpose, to uplift the home. The refrigerator had a magnetic to do list pad on its surface. "fruits" "vegetables" "olive oil" "balsamic vinegar." He searched the cabinets, looking for coffee filters and coffee. He finally found them and proceeded to make some coffee. He looked for a mug and noticed that all the dishware was white. He poured it into a large white mug and added some cream and sugar. Then he headed for Helena's bedroom.

He set the coffee on her bedside table and stared at her while she was asleep. Everyone always looked their best when they were asleep, so peaceful, he thought. He gently nudged her arm.

"Helena."

She stirred.

"Helena."

She opened her eyes. He took the coffee and held it out to her.

"I made you some coffee."

She sat up in bed and ran her hand through her hair. Her eyes were puffy from crying.

"Oh, thank you." She took the mug and sipped carefully.

"How are you feeling?"

"OK. Better." She smiled.

They stared at each other and knew what was on each other's mind. They weren't sure how to address it. It was Tom who finally spoke.

"Listen, about what you asked me last night…"

"Look, Tom, I'm *really* sorry. You don't have to do anything you don't want to do. You don't owe me anything."

"No, I do have to do something," he said. "But…I have to think about it. I can't deal with all this right now. You're going to have to give me some time. And just so you know, I'm not going to see Elise."

"You aren't?"

"No."

It was almost daybreak and the sun peeked through the window, melting off the early morning clouds. Helena got out of bed. She was still wearing her clothes from the night before.

Tom stood up and thought about touching her, taking her hands in his, gently sweeping her hair from her face, hugging her. But he didn't. Without speaking, Tom gathered his coat and headed for the door.

"Talk you later."

"Bye."

Tom took a deep breath of the early morning air as he left Helena's home. His car was waiting for him at the curbside and he took out his keys.

He climbed in his car and sped home. Luckily, the freeways were clear and he arrived at the Herald in time for work.

He walked in and said hello to the receptionist. Then he made his way to his desk. He turned on his computer and scrolled through his e-mails. He realized that he was hungry and hadn't eaten breakfast, so he went to the break room to get a breakfast bar from the vending machine and a coffee. He ran into Elise in the break room, and, after hearing about everything from Helena last night began to see her in a different light.

"Good morning!" she proclaimed.

"Morning," he replied.

Elise immediately suspected that something was wrong.

"What's the matter?" she asked.

"Nothing. I'm just tired, that's all."

Elise was stirring her coffee and threw the stir stick in the garbage. She took a sip and asked whether he wanted to join her and a few staffers for lunch today. Tom tried not to appear annoyed.

"Actually, I think I'm going to try and save some money and eat at home today."

"Oh, okay," Elise said, disappointed. "We're probably going to go to this great Japanese place right around the corner."

"Yeah, no, that's okay. I think I'll pass today. Thanks for the invite, though."

Balancing his coffee in one hand so as not to spill it, he made his way out of the break room and back to his desk.

The day went by slowly, it was probably the slowest day Tom had yet experienced. All he wanted to do was go home and sleep for a while, and then he wanted to sit and really think about this whole situation he got dragged into.

When the clock finally hit 5:30, Tom sighed with relief and immediately turned off his computer. He threw on his coat and left. Elise noticed him leaving and exhaled in frustration. She wondered why he had turned off to her so suddenly. She had even written him a couple of emails and did not receive any replies. She had written: Not your usual self, u ok? No answer. Can I buy you a drink after work? No response.

Tom took the long way home and stopped by the liquor store for a pack of cigarettes. He opened them up and lit one, inhaling slowly and staring absently out the front windshield of his car, waiting at a red light. He didn't usually smoke, but he was feeling stressed and confused. He needed some kind of release. He finally made it home. The entire time he had thought about what happened the night before with Helena. He had to admit he was thankful for the job she secured for him at the newspaper. He recognized that her intentions were good, albeit a bit off. He didn't think she was the type to be so obsessive, but she was definitely overly emotional what with all the crying and weeping. She was a completely different person at work. Not the Helena he thought he knew. But he felt softness for her, he saw in her vulnerability, her need to be protected and truly loved. Elise, on the other hand, was more confident. She was sly and cunning. He didn't respect her anymore for what she had done to Helena. Even though the scheme was conjured up by the both of them, and was manipulative and shrewd, he also couldn't help but feel somewhat flattered at all the time and attention they spent brewing up this plan.

He sat on his couch and put his feet on his small leather ottoman. He thought about what to say to Helena, and what to do about the situation. Elise did not know that Helena had told him about the whole scheme, and he wanted to keep it that way.

∾

It was Monday when Tom decided to make a visit to managing editor Paul Schlabely.

"Hello sir, can I talk to you for a moment?"

"Sure, Tom, isn't it?"

"Yes."

"What can I help you with?"

"Well, I'm new here, as you know, and I have a grievance with one of your editors – Elise Rudolph?"

"Yes, what's wrong, Tom?"

"Well, I've been receiving a lot of personal emails from her at work, and invitations to lunch and dinner, and I was wondering if that was normal around here. I'm feeling a little uncomfortable with her overly excessive attention."

"Are you accusing her of harassment?"

"No, no, not exactly –"

"Because we run a very professional establishment here, all our editors and staffers are trained and quite aware of the law –"

"Oh, I'm sure, sir, I'm sure you're correct, and I'm not questioning your establishment here. I just wanted to bring it to your attention."

"Well, okay. Do you have any evidence of this so called 'attention'?"

Tom placed a pile of emails on his desk. A large, fat man, Paul Shlabley took them in his sausage-like fingers and began to sift through them.

"Most of these seem like friendly e-mails to the new recruit. I don't see why you're so distressed."

"Well, if that's what you think sir, I'll just leave it at that."

"I'll tell you what, let's give this a few more days, and if the emails keep coming, you print them out and let me know."

"OK, thank you for your time sir. I appreciate it." Tom stood up and reached over the desk to shake his hand. Then he left the office.

He walked back to his desk, and passed Elise on the way.

"How's it going?" she called out.

"Great," he replied.

When he returned to his desk, he noticed the e-mail sign flashing in the corner. He pulled up his mail and saw it was from Elise.

Need you to stay after to help research a story today.

He wrote back: **OK.** Send.

He really wasn't in the mood to stay late, but at the same time, he welcomed opportunities to do things other than sort mail and answer phones. It was a busy day, and Tom got caught in the thick of it. Before he knew it, it was late afternoon. Tom took a short trip into the break room for a Coke and then went and hung out in the foyer, looking at all the framed photos. He looked out the glass doors and saw the setting sun retreating into the clouds. He lost himself in the sky, just for a few moments, and thought about Helena. As he stood there, he imagined her face, a mirage in the hazy blue stillness of the dusk quickly approaching. He wondered what she might be doing this very moment. He found himself wanting to go home to her, hold her, be with her. That's when he knew, he had made his decision. He hadn't realized how long he had been standing there in the foyer. He saw the receptionist's back to him further down the hallway. Someone entered through the double glass doors. Joe, a reporter, was holding two plastic bags. The pungent smell of food hit Tom's nostrils and he could only guess this was dinner for everyone staying late.

"Hey, guy," Joe greeted him.

"Chinese?"

"No, Mexican."

Tom wondered why no one had asked him what he wanted, since he, too, was staying late. He thought of asking Joe, but at the last minute, decided against it.

He waited for Joe to disappear down the hallway, and then began trekking his way back to the newsroom. He stuck out his hand and ran his fingers over the walls as he walked. He entered the newsroom and went to Elise's office. She was already digging in to her dinner. He peered in and knocked lightly on the door, which was halfway open.

"Come on in." Elise looked up.

"Have a seat."

Tom sat down in front of her, the same way he had when she had given him the fake interview. He thought back, the headhunter e-mail, the phone conversations, the hiring – all of it had been fake!

He couldn't help but feel momentarily duped, tricked, made a fool of, a pawn in someone's sick game. He felt ill. He drank his Coke and stared at Elise, trying not to look angry and judgmental. This was just as bad as if someone had gotten hired because of the way she looked, but it wasn't exactly along those same lines, because Helena had really believed she was doing something good. He had to admit, if Elise had not interfered, Helena could have gotten away with it. He would have forgiven her because she was really trying to help, and she had used her resources to her advantage. The only thing at risk was a broken heart. Who's saying that *he* would fall in love with *her*? Did she think getting him a foot in the door was enough to cement an automatic relationship? It was a little naïve, but bold. Tom continued to sip his soda and watched Elise eat.

"I'll be at my desk when you need me."

"Wait, Tom, sheesh, have you been acting strange lately. I need you to do some research in the library on Gary Langley, he's the district rep. for Sun Valley. We're doing profiles of the candidates and the issues for elections. There should be some info other than what you might find in a search engine in the library. I'll meet you there in ten minutes."

"OK." Tom answered bluntly. He made his way to the library, and began sifting through files. He found some old articles and fished them out. Then he saw Elise who came in to the library and shut the door.

"I found these articles – "

"Tom, we need to talk."

Tom paused. Oh no, he thought. A rehash of the night with Helena flashed before him.

"I don't know what happened in the last couple of days, but I just want you to know that I went through a lot, and I'm not going to go into detail, to get you here to work for us, and frankly, I don't see any problem in getting someone else if you happen to be unhappy with my leadership – "

"Woa, wait a second," Tom stepped back and stared into her eyes, penetrating her equally hard gaze. "I don't think I've done anything to show that I'm unhappy aside from reject the many *advances* that I've been receiving from you ever since I got hired here!"

"And who was the one who couldn't keep his hands off me at brunch that day?"

"I was drunk! And the night we first kissed I was drunk!"

"Are you saying you don't like me?"

"No, I mean, yes. Actually –"

"Because I put you here, and unless I'm happy with you, I can easily take you out."

"Are you saying – "

"You know what I'm saying." Elise picked up the articles and threw them down. "Photocopy these, and give them to Mary." She looked at him one last time and left the library.

Tom looked at the articles on the table. He shook his head in disgust and sat down.

Later that night, Tom couldn't sleep. When he finally did, he kept having terrible nightmares. He woke up in the middle of the night and sat at his kitchen table. He couldn't believe what Elise had said to him. What was happening was definitely wrong, but how could he bring this to Shlabely's attention when he didn't really have hard proof, other than the "friendly" e-mails? Then he remembered, Shlabely had told him that if the e-mails continued after that day, he should print them out and speak to him again. They had, what with her questioning him about his mood, asking him what was wrong, and then offering to buy him a drink after work. Tom was elated at the prospect of getting Elise reprimanded. Better yet, though, he wanted her gone, so he could work in peace. What he originally had thought of her began to morph. Her "confidence" and "aggression" could now be seen as "pushy" and "bossy." Her face was not one of smart self-reliance, but one of conniving manipulation. Underneath her sharp business suits and self-assured gait was a woman unabashed and insecure. The paper would be better without her, in his opinion. Joe could replace her, or Stan, or even Mary. He didn't know the hierarchy just yet, maybe they would even have to replace her from the outside. Whatever they had to do, Tom would be behind it.

∞

The very next day, Tom got to work early and wasted no time in fulfilling his agenda he had made roughly the night before. No one was in the newsroom and he immediately, scrolled through his e-mails and printed out the ones sent to him after he had first spoken to Shlabley. He gathered them together and stapled them. Then he worked on an assignment until he saw Shlabely walk in.

"How you doing, Tom?"

"Good, thanks, how are you this morning?"

"Not bad," he answered. He ran his hand over his balding head and straightened his cuffs. Then as Shlabely headed toward his office, Tom stood up with the e-mails in hand and went after him.

"Uh, sir, Mr. Shlabely? I'd like to talk to you if you have a minute. In private."

Paul Shlabely turned around and looked at Tom.

"You can't keep away from me lately, can you? OK, come on into my office."

"Thank you."

Tom sat down across from the Sun Valley Herald executive editor and tried to remain calm.

"What can I do for you, son."

"Well, remember a few days ago, I told you I was feeling uncomfortable about one of your editors, Elise Rudolph?"

"Yes, I do remember."

"Well, I had shown you some personal e-mails that she had written me ever since I started working, and I told you that I was uncomfortable with her excessive attention.

"Uh huh."

"You told me that if I continued to receive e-mails from her *after* that day, that I should print them out and speak with you. Well, I did receive two emails and I have reason to believe that she specifically told me that if I made her unhappy, she could easily fire me," Tom paused, then he added,

"That's a direct quote."

"Let me see those, Tom." He looked through the e-mails, just as he did the first time and sighed.

"Well, it does appear that she has an overt interest in you. Now you were saying that she told you something in person?"

"Yes, she told me that "if I made her unhappy" she could easily "take me out." And I might add that she told me this after I began rejecting her invitations."

"And when and where did she tell you this?"

"In the library yesterday. We were alone."

"Hmm…" Paul Shlabely smoothed his brow. "I don't know what to tell you Tom. Elise hasn't been with us for that long, but we respect her work and she does a good job for us."

"Well, I'm sorry to be the bearer of bad news, but she's not what you think. I also have reason to believe that she personally orchestrated the exodus of the former news clerk."

"What? Now come on, Tom. You're grasping for straws now. Chester made a very serious mistake, it was unforgivable."

"Well, I do feel obligated to tell you what's going on. I'm not going to sit back and be a victim."

Shlabely looked at Tom grimly.

"OK, Tom. I'll see what I can do."

Tom stood up and left the office.

He ran into Elise on the way out and nearly jumped in surprise. Seeing her now was like seeing a ghost, some kind of cruel demon that he was trying to exorcize out of his system.

"Hello, Tom."

"Hello, Elise."

Tom moved swiftly past her and back to his desk. He didn't want to look back to see if she was going to Shlabely's office. He didn't want to look suspicious.

"Good morning Paul."

"Elise, just the person I wanted to see."

"Really?" Elise became suspicious.

"Sit down for a moment." Elise sat down.

Paul looked at her through his eyeglasses, the fluorescent light hit them causing a sheen that distorted his eyes behind them. He licked his lips and spoke causing the jowls around his mouth to flap subtly, making his seem, for a moment, like a bulldog.

"I have reason to believe that you have taken a personal interest in one of your underlings here."

"I'm sorry?"

"Yes, this Tom character. He claims that you've been making advances toward him. He even has gone so far as to say that you threatened to fire him if he 'made you unhappy.'"

Elise stared at him in disbelief.

"Paul, I did nothing of the kind. I have done nothing but encourage him and support him since he started working here."

"Hmm. I know you well, Elise, I think these e-mails you have been sending have been a little out of character for you."

"He gave you my e-mails? Those were just innocent banter. Are you accusing me of harassing him?"

"Well, according to these e-mails, you have been writing him every day sometimes two or three times a day."

"Well, I likened myself to be something of a mentor…"

"Elise. Drop the act. I know a situation when I see it. This kid is not a bad looking guy. Now, you asked me to trust you in hiring a replacement for Chester. What's going on?"

"Paul. Tom happened to be in the right place at the right time. I'm not after him."

"These e-mails have got to stop, because he told me that you are making him uncomfortable."

"OK. Fine. I guess some people just don't know when you are trying to be helpful."

"Listen Elise, keep this situation in check please, I don't want to have to baby sit you both."

"I understand."

Elise left Shlabely and went to her office. She was furious. She closed the door and sat at her desk. She looked around as if looking for something to throw. She couldn't find anything.

"Argh!" She cried out. She took a deep breath, straightened her shirt and jacket and turned on her computer. She just then realized that she hadn't been in communication with Helena for days. Sometimes they would both get so busy, but they always found time to make a phone call or drop an e-mail. It hadn't bothered her until now, because she was angry and wanted to spew to Helena, but she couldn't, because Helena (as far as she knew) had no idea what was going on with her and Tom. Now, Tom had gone from mad crush to worst enemy. One part of her felt like sabotaging him, but she just couldn't do that. She felt a soft spot for him and though she hated to admit it, her feelings for him hadn't really changed. This made her angrier and more confused. She was stuck.

Tom went through his day and remained busy. He ran around the newsroom, assisting in the elections coverage. There had also been a fire and a car accident that had happened simultaneously and he was assigned to do a couple of candidate interviews to cover for a reporter. He was happy to be getting more writing assignments. He looked around and took a moment to enjoy the frenetic pace before moving on to the next task.

Elise sat at her desk quietly. She felt paralyzed. Maybe she would call Helena and tell her everything. She knew deep inside that the reason why she felt so bad was the fact that she was keeping these secrets and going after Tom behind Helena's back. But she still couldn't get herself to do it. She couldn't own up to her mistakes. She just wanted it to go away. She wanted life to be the way it was before Tom came onto the scene, before Helena had asked her to do all these favors. She wanted to go back to the time when she knew what was right and wrong, and she was safe and secure in her job. Tom was meddling with her career. He had gone too far.

14

~

Elise knew that once you were labeled as a certain "type," people would forever cast you in that light, but she had the penchant of seeing the world as smaller than it actually was. She saw the media industry as a "small world," and a friend had told her once, "Don't kid yourself." But she still believed it. Maybe she was kidding herself, maybe she saw herself as just that much more important than the next person because she got to see her name in print. She didn't know for sure, but she felt she knew enough. She knew that if anyone found out about her tendency to rely a little too heavily on substances just to get through the day, or to shake off normal every day stressors, she would be devastated – she had to remain calm and in control in her appearances.

Her mother was an ordinary housewife, her father – a cheery and handsome man who chain-smoked Pall Malls and died of a heart attack when she was 19. She loved her father dearly, and although already out of the house and well into her college years, she felt a huge gaping hole that got wider when he left. Her mother, bored and, she believed, neglected, had never been very kind to her. She often took out her anger on Elise, sometimes, they fought to the point of shoving matches, but it never escalated to blows. Her father, a real estate salesman, was much more warm and loving. As an only child, things were very normal and Elise remembered being very happy, but it only lasted up to her teenage years, which was when her mother started drinking a little too much and passing out when she could have been spending time with her daughter. Her father stayed out later and later, and when he came home, he was often drunk and he and her mother fought. Her mother accused him of having an affair, which he adamantly denied. He took longer and longer business trips; Elise's mother grew more and more depressed. Elise told herself that she would never end up like her mother, that she would go to college and try to be something, and she wanted to write. So far, her goals had been fulfilled.

But in matters of the heart, it was quite a different case. She went through a number of failed relationships, one after another. She couldn't seem to understand what went wrong. She realized that she was incapable of true intimacy and thought that arguing meant closeness, disclosure, a kind of therapy. You tell me what's wrong with me, and I'll tell you what's wrong with you. Then we can get close and we're all the better for it – a sort of constructive criticism for the soul. It never worked, and when her partners would slowly pull away and leave, she was left alone, again, pondering her fate.

But she never talked about her relationships with anyone, except Helena. Even with Helena, she talked superficially, telling her about the what and the where, but never the how and the why. Then she would take a few days or weeks to recover, and move on. Helena was the opposite, droning on and on about her relationships and wondering what went wrong, wanting Elise to help her psychoanalyze it. Elise was not like that; one might fear she would one day become completely emotionally detached. But her relationships, in private, were high drama. Arguing was very emotionally draining and it happened because she cared. She cared enough to beg the questions, demand the answers and uncover where she stood. She was often so intense, her relationships would just spontaneously combust. She often failed to see it until it was too late.

People could see that about Elise. They were attracted to her intensity, as Tom was. Her colleagues were attracted to it. She made it this far in her career because of it. She was, in her own "small world," a success.

෨

In another world away, Helena was pondering her own fate with Tom. It had been three days since their conversation and she was wondering what she should do. Should she call him, or wait for him to call her? She couldn't stop thinking about that night, the way he looked, when he had held her and she had felt that same electricity and heat that she felt during his first few days at Advent. Everything seemed that much more real to her since he was only a half hour away, and not a thousand miles away. It made her want to jump in her car and go see him, but she felt that would be too forward. She would just have to sit and wait. Wait for her destiny as her friend Chaz would have told her. If it was meant to be it would happen. But as soon as she thought it, Helena stopped herself and remembered she was trying to go against that old advice. It was up to her to take action. She couldn't just sit on her hands and wait. She picked up the phone and paused.

"Helena? They need you in the conference room." Tony, a co-worker, poked his head into her office.

Helena jumped slightly and put the phone back in its receiver.

"OK, I'll be right there."

She sent off a couple of e-mails and then made her way to the conference room. It was a conference call with all the managers to discuss the fourth quarter strategy. She had forgotten all about it because her mind had been on Tom. She quickly remembered the e-mails that had been sent to her and tried to prepare herself in two minutes. Luckily, they handed out copies and got started. Helena read over them quickly. Then the meeting started.

On her way out after the meeting had ended, she had noticed one of the managers, Rick, looking at her. She never gave him much mind, but she felt he was paying more attention to her than usual. She looked at him and their eyes locked. He smiled at her and nodded.

"Hello, Helena."

"Hi, Rick."

They paused for a moment until Rick finally spoke.

"Would you like to join me for lunch?"

"Sure. Let me just go back to my office for my purse."

Helena made her way to her office and then met Rick in the hallway.

"Where would you like to go?" he asked.

"Anywhere. How about the corner deli?"

"Sounds great."

They took the elevator to the ground floor and walked outside. It was a breezy, balmy day with a slight overcast. They arrived at the deli and ordered. It was crowded, mostly men and women in suits, from other offices, also on lunch break. They couldn't find a table, so they went to sit down outside on a bench. They were surrounded by concrete and sky-rises, but there were a lot of places to sit down. Architecturally, the area was built with concrete surrounding gardens of bushes and fountains, where many others sat, eating out of lunch bags or using the concrete as their table. There were also many tables set up outside the indoor mall filled with places to eat, including a chocolate confectionary shop, where they made Helena's favorite, apples covered with brown and white chocolate rolled in cracked candies or nuts.

As they sat on the bench, pigeons landed near them searching for food.

"So how's your sandwich?" Rick asked.

"Good. How's yours?"

"Delicious. Do you go to that deli often?"

"Yeah. It's healthier than McDonald's. Though I do crave a cheeseburger every now and then."

"I just got back from Chicago, they said this new guy they hired is having problems."

"Really?"

"Oh, he's just not understanding the computer system and he's having some trouble with people in the office."

"That new guy we hired. Mason Andrews. What do you think is wrong? I mean, I was there during the interview. He seemed fine. Kip was really for him."

"Well, they're thinking of canning him."

"Again?"

"You might have to take another trip."

"Well, maybe we should call the person we're thinking of in again this time. For a second interview."

"They want to send me with you."

"Oh. OK. We'll be partners then."

Helena looked at her watch. It was five until one.

"We better get going." She said.

"Yeah."

They made their way through the crowds and back to the office building. Rick lit a cigarette on the way back. He was a thin, tall man, with black hair cut neatly and smooth white skin. He had a thin nose and full lips, almost a feminine quality about him. She guessed that he was Korean, judging from is last name, Lee. Helena wouldn't call him unattractive, and he was a good manager. They had worked together for about five years now.

They got off on the 7th floor and went to their respective offices. After dropping off her purse, Helena went to the head manager, Grant Lukeheimer's, office.

"Got a minute?"

Grant Lukeheimer was on the phone with his mistress, but he pretended like it was a business call. He shooed her away, and Helena grimaced while she mouthed, "OK," and stood outside his office.

Grant turned around in his chair so his back faced the doorway and murmured under his breath.

"I miss you too, I know, I know, I will soon. I've got to go now."

"Helena!" he boomed. "Come on in."

Helena walked in and sat down.

"Hi. I just wanted to know when you're shipping Rick and I out to Chicago."

"Ah, you heard."

"Rick told me."

"OK, probably in the next few days. Gerard is thinking of giving this Mason guy the boot tomorrow. I just got off the phone with him."

"OK. So soon, then."

"Yes, but I'll let you know."

"OK. Thanks, Grant."

He waved her out and turned back to his computer.

∽

Elise sat at her desk going through files on her computer and sending emails. She noticed that Tom was going out on frequent breaks outside, probably to smoke. Sometime after lunch, she saw him get up again to make his way out of the building to the outdoor patio. This time, she followed him.

Sure enough, Tom was lighting a cigarette when he saw Elise come through the door. She stared at him with her arms folded across her chest, leaning against a table. He felt the urge to be sarcastic. Her presence annoyed him, and her glare transfixed upon him like an interrogator's light in some South American prison.

"Can I help you?" he asked, taking the cigarette from his mouth and blowing out the smoke slowly.

"Do you think I'm joking with you?" Elise retorted sharply.

"Joking about what?"

"You went to Shlabley about me? You're telling him I'm harassing you?"

"Well, you did."

Elise snorted and stared at him incredulously.

"Did you or did you not threaten me in the library two days ago?"

"You know, Shlabely is a busy man, and he knows me, he's not going to put up with your whining."

"Am I whining?"

"Yes, you are."

Tom laughed. It was a genuine deep, hearty, high-pitched laughter that came from the pit of his stomach, something he rarely did. It was a laugh at someone out of ridicule and not because something was simply funny in a comedic kind of way. Nor was it a laugh to politely accompany uncomfortable conversation, made at stupid jokes or to break the ice during some kind of scenario done for political reasons or to ease others' at the obvious discomfort of, say, a party where no one knew each other; that kind of fake laughter at absolutely nothing.

Elise's eyes welled up in embarrassment. She didn't know what more she could do. She felt helpless and desperate, and she wasn't quite sure why. She felt the urge to go home and cry, maybe have a drink and call a friend. But of course, her best friend was no longer.

"Listen, this is my *job* we're talking about. You messing with my job is a serious offense, in my eyes."

"Shlabely isn't stupid, he'll see who is telling the truth in the end." Tom threw his cigarette on the floor and mashed it with his shoe before standing up.

Elise watched as Tom slipped past her and went back into the building. She stared at the floor for what seemed like several minutes before the tears started to flow. She wiped her eyes delicately with her manicured acrylic fingers, and then, afraid someone might see her, almost ran into the building and to the bathroom. There, she found an empty stall and sat down before she really started sobbing. The tears came and came, her shoulders shook as she covered her face with her hands. It went on for almost 15 minutes before she finally stopped. She came out of the restroom and splashed some water on her face. Her eyes were puffy and swollen, if anyone asked her what was wrong, she would just have to tell them she was having a bad day. She left the restroom and went back to her desk. She rummaged through her purse and found some vicodin. Then she went to the break room and swallowed it down with some water. She tried to move quickly, so that no one would stop her in the news room. Luckily, no one did, and she retreated into her small office and shut the door. She wanted to be alone. She couldn't face anybody right now.

She wanted to go home early, but she knew that was impossible. She had so much to do. She could soon feel the pills working their way through her system and she began to feel calmer. She went through her workload in a pleasant haze of drugged serenity, not too sleepy, not too stressed, just right. She soon engaged in her work, forgetting about Tom and the altercation that had just happened an hour ago. She looked forward to going home, dinner, and sleep. Staffers began knocking on her door, and her phone started to ring. She threw herself into her responsibilities and when she spoke, it was with such quiet clarity, it surprised her from her angry tirade that could have escalated into something much worse, with Tom on the patio. She conducted herself as she usually did, and she was sure nobody suspected anything different about her.

She walked past Tom on her way out for the evening with no acknowledgement of any kind, and, as far as she was concerned, he was non-existent. She drove home lazily, smoking and listening to NPR. The voices soothed her, as she listened intently, picking up pieces of information and then discarding them randomly in her mind. Her mind began to loosen somewhat, like a puzzle or a brick that would break off into dried sand at the touch of someone's hand. She turned into her driveway and turned off the engine. She dragged herself out of the car and stumbled, falling to her knees on the hard concrete. It hurt, but she did not express any sentiment of pain. She picked herself up clumsily and walked toward her door. She entered the house and threw her keys on the table. Her cat began to meow intensely and it started to alarm her. She soon realized that she had no food in her bowl. She filled up the bowl and went straight to the refrigerator without taking off her shoes or her jacket. She threw a frozen Lean Cuisine in the microwave and uncorked a bottle of red wine. She poured herself a glass and drank it quickly. She poured herself another glass and sipped it, waiting for her dinner. She ate her meal slowly, staring blindly through the glass kitchen table. She finished the entire bottle of wine and then stumbled into her bedroom where she stripped off her clothes and threw them to the floor, and all over her room, in the closet, on her bed. She crawled into bed naked. She lay there for quite a while, her thoughts swimming and floating in the drug-induced stupor. It didn't take long before she finally fell asleep, or, more appropriately, passed out.

Elise woke up crying. It was the middle of the night. She grabbed a pillow and noticed she was naked. She got up and flipped on the light, before looking for her pajamas. She found an old nightie and then flipped off the light and crawled back into bed. She was still crying. Her head was pounding, but she felt too immobilized to get an aspirin. She lied there on her back and suffered, as tears flowed down the sides of her face and filled her ears. Her nose filled with mucus. She stuffed her face in the pillow and bawled, loudly. It lasted all night. She couldn't stop crying. What would she do about work tomorrow? She would have to call in sick. She was coming undone, slowly. This was temporary, she told herself, you'll get over this. Things could be much worse.

She called in sick the next day, and the next. She finally told Shlabely that she was having a personal crisis.

"We don't deal with 'personal crises' here, Elise. Either you're sick and you take a day or two to recover, or you're not and you come in, we don't handle mid-life crises on our clock."

Elise dragged herself to work the next day feeling like she had been mauled by tigers. Her entire body hurt and she was nursing terrible hangovers. She did what she could at work without getting too involved in the emotional train wreck that was just across the office called Tom Overton. She hated him. It was then that Elise began to lose her senses. He was a tease, he was a smug, pretty boy with rich parents who had been spoon fed all his life and was trying to break into *her* field. He didn't belong here. She could drop him – she stopped herself. No, she could not. He had beaten her to the punch - going to Shlabely. Now, Shlabely had reason to believe she *might* have had an interest in him. And that altogether was in some ways, inappropriate, unless the other's feelings are mutual. But he had turned off to her, and she didn't know why. She began to resent him. *He* had used *her*! He had cozied his way right into her heart and then, as soon as things became secure and comfortable for him, he dropped her like an egg from a hen. She couldn't believe his audacity. The nerve. Maybe he even wanted her position, or wanted someone else in it. She had seen him talking to Hal, one of the long-time writers on the city desk. Perhaps they had something up their sleeves. How would she know? She began to feel prickly all over, and cold, almost as if she were naked. Every nerve felt exposed, and raw. She needed something, like a blanket or a jacket. She stared absent-mindedly at her computer screen, reading but not comprehending. She began to correlate Tom with the essence of evil, someone cunning, sly, manipulative. She leaned back in her chair until she caught a glimpse of him across the way; he was surely plotting against her.

15

~

Helena and Rick landed in Chicago on an early flight, and it was Rick who suggested they go grab some dinner. They went to a Mediterranean restaurant near the hotel that appeared busy so they assumed it must be very popular. When they finally got a table, Helena was surprised when Rick pulled out her chair for her as if they were on a date. They ordered and made small talk, but soon the conversation turned personal, and Rick was asking her about her family and musical tastes. She went along politely, she began to see how engaging he was and soon they were laughing like old friends.

"I'm glad you don't mind Mediterranean, some people don't like to try anything except the usual favorites, like Japanese, Mexican or Chinese."

"Oh, no, I'm willing to try anything once."

"So do you get to see your parents often? Being from the East coast?"

"Once in a while, for holidays. My mother is on her last leg, I worry about her. My dad passed away when I was in high school."

"Oh, I'm sorry," Helena said, taking a bite of falefel.

"Yeah, well, he was a heavy smoker. Cancer."

Rick noticed Helena wincing.

"I haven't seen you taking smoke breaks outside lately," he said. "Did you quit?"

"Actually, yeah, I'm trying to. Oh, you're not supposed to say 'trying.' They say to be resolute, so yes, I Have Quit."

"Wow, great. Good for you. I try, but, I just can't seem to shake it."

She asked him if he tried the gum, patch, etc. He said he had tried everything.

"Well, maybe you could go to those Nicotines Anonymous meetings," Helena offered.

"That's one thing I haven't tried yet."

"Would you like to go together sometime?"

"Yeah, that might not be a bad idea."

At the end of their meal, they ordered some ice coffee and continued to talk. They conversed without one dominating the other. In many conversations, there is usually a talker, and then there is a listener. Rick and Helena spoke in equal time, exchanging information equally. When they finally returned to their hotel, Rick awkwardly reached out to her and gave her a hug. They looked at each other and then smiled.

"Good night."

"Good night. See you tomorrow."

Helena felt as though she had just been on a very nice date. They walked back to the hotel and parted ways in the lobby, after agreeing to meet there the next morning.

Helena walked to her room and entered with her room key. She went inside and sat on her bed. She found herself smiling, and she felt warm.

Then she realized that she hadn't thought about Tom in nearly 48 hours.

∾

Helena slept well that night, feeling something she hadn't felt in a long time, at peace with herself. She had forgotten what it felt like to have a genuine conversation with someone, feeling good about a type of disclosure that was sort of the type you might have being in therapy without the often off-putting self-realizing input of the therapist. Sometimes it happened with complete strangers, but most of the time it happened with an acquaintance. It was a nice feeling getting to know someone; it felt fresh and stimulating. Not only that, but Rick had somehow tapped into her long lost ability to relax and enjoy herself with a member of the opposite sex. She wondered how it could have happened so aptly, right under her nose, without her catching on to some kind of discomfort. It felt natural, and it made her feel good.

∾

The next morning, Helena awoke feeling refreshed from a good night's sleep. She went through her morning routine, reminding herself that she had kept her vow to quit smoking and had not for nearly one month now. She met Rick in the lobby and they jetted off to the Chicago office to take care of the new hire.

They interviewed only a few candidates, and made their decision quickly. This time, Rick had made a hefty amount of input and for the first time Helena felt guilty having tampered with the hiring process with Tom. In a way, all this re-hiring had inadvertently been caused by that incident, though no one but her knew it. She kept somewhat quiet during the process this time, letting Rick take over. She would be glad when this was all over.

Rick Lee was surprised at Helena's demeanor during the hiring process. She was usually much more vocal and pro-active. He interpreted it as having gotten the best of her, perhaps she had caught on to his admiration of her and was letting him take the lead because she was impressed. He had had his eye on her for some time now, but was too afraid to approach her. Though it may not have exhibited itself at work, he was really sort of a shy person in his personal life, and had not but only a handful of relationships in his life. But he had really enjoyed having dinner with her, and it was really sort of fate that he had been scheduled to go on this trip with her. It wasn't as if he had planned it or anything – Grant had decided that. He could only look at it as a hopeful sign that maybe he could have a chance at getting to know her.

The day ended before they knew it, and they had all finally agreed on a new associate. Afterwards, as they were packing up to leave, Rick was glad when Helena asked him to join her for dinner again. Not wanting to seem overeager, he accepted graciously.

16

~

Elise's breakfast rumbled up through her throat and into the clean white basin of the toilet bowl. Her body shook with spasms. This reverse peristalsis was not lost on Elise, who quickly realized that her various stressors were showing themselves physically, and if she did not do something soon, she would be a very sick person. She dropped to her knees and hugged the basin. She was stiff with fear that one of her co-workers would walk in the bathroom, recognize that someone was hacking uncontrollably and then later wait outside to see who emerged. She didn't put it past her staff to do something of the kind. She had to finish up quickly. It lasted another five minutes or so and then she stood up and flushed the putrid contents of her stomach and watched the pools of spittle and chunks of her eggs and toast disappear down the swirling water shaft that led to the dank sewage below. She emerged from the stall and rinsed her mouth out, gargled and looked at herself in the mirror. Her eyes were red and watery, most of her makeup had come off. She looked like hell. She tried to dab her eyes and put some powder on her face and around her eyes to cover up the redness. She didn't bother with any mascara or eye shadow, just a little bit of lipstick, so as not to appear completely dead, though that was how she felt. She was numbed by her drinking the night before, which was becoming a dangerous habit lately. She usually had a glass of wine or a beer once a night, but now she was far past her usual number along with adding a few highballs, which of course explained her need to run to the bathroom to extricate herself from the subdued pain of the contents of her stomach swirling in a cacophonous mix of vodka (or rum, depending on her mood), beer and wine.

She had been like this for days. She wasn't sure how much longer she could go on. They needed her in the newsroom. She needed Tom Overton to disappear. She had been avoiding him, and he had been avoiding her. It was like living with someone you couldn't stand and both of you knew it, so you tried to avoid each other like the plague but you couldn't help but run into one another from time to time, at which point there was an unspoken tension that kept each person in fear of the other breaking that silence.

One good thing, though, was that they seemed to respect each other's mutual hatred for each other, allowing for looks to communicate their intense dislike before it escalated into openly snide remarks. For these two, angry silence was the daily special.

∾

"Never dip your pen in the company ink."

"Yeah, but it happens all the time. No one listens to those stupid modern-day proverbs, much less heeds them."

Helena was talking to Coleen, relationship guru extraordinaire. Actually, she was just a college friend come manicurist.

"You think he's cute?"

"No, that picture you have of him kind of looks weird. He reminded me of a weasel."

"But you have never dated an Asian guy. And he's Korean."

"I kind of like him. Something about him is sweet and unassuming."

"What about the love of your life aka Tom?"

Helena suddenly froze. She remembered what had happened the night of her "confession." She hadn't talked to Tom since then. Truthfully, she had been procrastinating, feeling both embarrassed at the seriousness with which they had handled such a scheme and grateful that he had not reacted with absolute disgust and hatred.

"Well," she lied, "I'm kind of over him."

"So soon?"

Coleen didn't know the whole story. It was far too long and complicated to discuss over the 20-minutes it took to do nails. She just didn't want to get into it. Coleen was prone to pop psychology psychobabble and had a penchant for comparing real life scenarios to mediocre big money chick flicks that churned out the old and tired themes like "dump the loser and get a life," or "if you don't act now you'll regret it later," or "demand respect, don't take his shit," or, as Barbara Streisand so aptly put it "all is fair in love and war." Helena sighed heavily, so be it.

Hence, Helena chose to stay tight-lipped about the details.

"Yeah, let's just say he was out of my league."

Coleen paused and looked up at Helena.

"It should be the other way around."

∾

When Helena returned home, she thought good and hard about what her next move should be. She hadn't heard from Elise for nearly a week. She hadn't returned any of her calls or e-mails. While Helena scratched her head wondering what had happened to her best friend, Tom was busy at work spinning in his position as a glorified administrative assistant.

"This is bullshit," muttered Tom under his breath. Why the heck was he here? What was he doing with his life? He had a law degree and had dropped a $50,000 a year salary in management consulting just to jump on the "sensitive artist" bandwagon that his friends from the art school at University of Connecticut seemed so content on. He had a girlfriend from the department (it was a short-lived albeit passionate romance – she was his fling, and he was her "inspiration" for her next project – an installation canvassing the ups and downs of heterosexual sex, which, being bisexual, she claimed was "almost entirely fake and insincere"). She eventually ended up in a psychiatric ward after suffering an intense breakdown shortly before graduation (it was only for a few days). Anyway, her friends took an immediate liking for him, and he found himself drowning in an elixir of free love and pretentious banter that eventually became clouded over with pot smoke and bottle after bottle of inexpensive merlot.

∾

Ely Johnson had plucked from the garden two roses. He snipped the stems and placed them in a shallow sugar bowl he had purchased at a church bazaar.

Tom scratched his head and adjusted his watch. The cursor on the computer screen in front of him blinked ominously. The phone rang.

"Hello?"

"Tom?"

"Yes."

"Hi, this is Helena."

"Oh, hello. How are you?"

"OK. Hanging in there, " Helena was biting her nail. "Listen, I feel like I have some unresolved issues about what I told you about that night."

"Yeah, well, I haven't put a whole lot of thought into it," he lied, thinking of the scheme he had tried to pull against Elise at work. He detested her. He wasn't really sure why, whether it was because she flirted with abuse of power, or because she had in a sense betrayed her best friend. He didn't want to tell Helena that, truthfully, he found their scheme both ridiculous and flattering. He noted a bit of anger and resentment, deep in the corners of his consciousness, and it made itself known when he made the quick decision to string Helena along, for how long, he didn't know. And it started as soon as he said:

"Would you like to have dinner sometime?"

Helena felt her stomach churn with anxiety. It was what she wanted to hear, in her dreams, she had fantasized time and time again of their eventual courtship, and the closer they got, the better it would be, and then, yes, the fated KISS, and a gush of warmth in her chest, a tingling all over her body.

"Yes," she accepted his proposal readily.

"How about this Friday – Wellington's? Off the freeway, I'll come get you, say about 7 p.m.?" He ran his hand through his hair. He was a little nervous, not quite sure what he was doing, but just wanted to…what was it that he wanted? He didn't quite know.

Ely Johnson. Who was Ely Johnson? Tom knew more than he was willing to explain. He shut off the computer and took off his clothes, getting ready to take a shower. He caught himself in the full-length mirror on his bedroom wall and studied his angles. The light was dim, only the desk light was on. He had a sparse smattering of hair on his chest and his legs looked abnormally skinny. It's easy to write about oneself, but how to not sound so self-indulgent? He stared at his reflection and lingered on his privates and then quickly averted his gaze upward until he landed on his clavicle. Someone had drawn a portrait of him once with charcoal, and he had marveled at the intensity of his eyes, a face that he had always thought as somewhat deadpan, had been brought to life by the artist, as if to tell him who he was. That he was not just a man, but a man with a history. He could see it, and it almost frightened him. He had lost the portrait, he believed, but it may be in his storage somewhere, he wasn't quite sure. It had hung on his college apartment wall for some time, but he got tired of seeing himself staring back at him and eventually took it down, rolled it up, secured it with a rubber band, and left it in his closet – to be found someday, to his surprise.

Wellington's? Why hadn't he suggested some-place more low-key? Wellington's was a steak house he had been to recently with his neighbor. It had dim lighting and high ceilings with crystal chandeliers, it had an aura of high class snobbery, but he had had a hankering for steak, and so when his neighbor, Jack, a FedEx delivery man with a penchant for going to the lake on weekends to collect driftwood, which he placed strategically around his house to create a feeling of being in nature, suggested Wellington's, Tom, hungry and a bit lonely, agreed.

"When you live in the heart of the city for as long as I have, you begin to crave the natural beauty of nature – mountains, rivers, forests, lakes," Jack had told him, justifying his driftwood collection.

"But we're in the suburbs," replied Tom.

"Yes, I am now, but I've just recently escaped the city. It can be mean and I decided I would stop being a glutton for punishment, that is, sacrificing my peace of mind, just to feel the fading romance of the city lights beyond my bedroom window and the minor convenience of walking to the 24-hour corner deli for a sandwich."

"Yeah, I do miss that, though," said Tom, as they waited for their hearty man's meal found only in a good t-bone.

If I take her there, it will mean that I really want to impress her, thought Tom. He wasn't quite sure whether he wanted to impress her or not. He realized that it was highly likely that something would transpire. It could be as simple as his being a marginally attractive male, and she being a marginally attractive female, and so one thing leads to another, as the story goes, usually with a few glasses of wine directing the show. Another fact he had on his side was that she had said she was "in love" with him, and so obviously, he had the upper hand, he philosophized. She'd do anything for him. It made him slightly uncomfortable, knowing how she felt about him, but he would have to investigate further, to see how exactly she operated. And so this Friday would be the beginning of Stage One: Getting Acquainted.

❧

Friday night. 5:00 p.m. Helena had been staring at the clock as it ticked by the minutes and the hours to her fated first date with Tom Overton. She paced in the kitchen, fixed herself a cup of tea, and now was watching the evening news. Work had been torture today, as her mind kept swirling with thoughts and scenarios of what might happen this evening. She hated Wellington's. She found the wait staff condescending. Whatever. She would survive another night of dinner there. She sipped her tea and stared absently at the television. A homicide in El Segundo and a car wreck on the freeway. No fires to report, not tonight. Tick, tick,

tick. 6:00 p.m. She had already taken a shower, and so now needed to start the primping. She dragged herself from the couch to the bathroom, feeling queasy, but trying to keep herself calm. She stared at herself in the bathroom mirror, let her hair out of the towel and began to blow dry. Her almond shaped eyes looked tired and smaller than usual, she would have to spend extra time opening them up with makeup – burgundy pencil, wine-berry eyeshadow, thick black mascara with special applicator wand. And not to forget the bags under those tired eyes, cover up and powder, soon her true ragged self would be concealed with a pat of powder and a flick of a brush. She slipped on sheer black hose and zipped up her dress. On went the jean jacket and black heels. Was jean too casual? For Wellington's, possibly. She peeled it off hastily and threw it on her bed. She chose a short wool jacket, and checked herself one last time in the mirror. Time: 6:35. So far, so good. She put on a coat of lip gloss, and then sat on her living room couch, and waited.

When the doorbell rang, she jumped. OK. This is it. Stay calm, be good. She opened the door and was greeted by a noseful of flowers. A mixed bouquet, but fragrant nonetheless.

"Hello," they both said, at the same time, rather carefully.

She took the bouquet after an awkward hug, and placed them on her dining table. That was, she admitted, gentlemanly, though somewhat old-fashioned. These days, men hardly ever gave flowers on a first date, unless it was prom night, that sort of formal "arrangement" that dictated what it might be like to go to some expensive ball in the heart of Nowhere, USA, where kids in jeans and flannel shirts exchanged such niceties for a night of "dress-up," only to end up in the back of a truck vomiting the last of the black cherry winecoolers they had paid some college guy to buy at the local pit-stop. Yes, that's romance for you.

She followed Tom out to his car, shivering slightly in the evening breeze. They headed over to Wellington's, and Helena found herself speechless, staring ahead at the series of streetlights they had to go through before hiking the ramp to the freeway, and entering Los Angeles proper. She didn't like venturing into the city too often. It reminded her of old history that she wanted to forget. She was trying to wipe the slate in her mind clean, so as not to allow judgment from her past experience cloud the present moment with, was he? Yes. The Man of Her Dreams.

It was something about him that she admired with awe. She wasn't quite sure how to explain it. He seemed self-assured, yet not cocky, level-headed, but with a tinge of rebelliousness. His golden hair was fine and trimmed neatly. Clean shaven, smooth skin. Quite handsome. Thin and svelte. Eyes of deep blue, intense and searching, sometimes even fearful. You could see the little boy inside, struggling to understand the world. She began to realize a pattern of men she was attracted to. Little boys, in men's bodies, pensive – a little dark, a little lonely, and almost desperate to hang on to their women, but feigning an act of indifference. She wanted to explore their hearts, understand what motivated them, their fears, their joys. It was a futile attempt however, to discover such buried truths, and so she anxiously stood by their side, usually to be tossed out carelessly because of her quiet respect, misinterpreted as growing dislike of him. But she knew he was different than the rest! She hoped he had a soul worth exploring, and she wanted to try harder this time to be more understanding of the male psyche. Here she was! With him! How it had all worked out! She would never let him go!

She remembered growing up in fear of her father, a stern, serious man who kept everything in check, under control. Things had to be just so, or someone would get it. It was not perfectionism, it was more a call for obedience. Her mother had it the worst, taking orders and receiving all the blame. Helena noticed it early on. It was a sadness, translated into weakness, literally, physically, where it seemed an effort to drag her body from the car to the front door. How she had at one time hated her father for being so tightly wound up. It was only later, when Helena had left them an empty nest, that they had somehow learned to live with each other's quirks, divorce was not an option. Separation for a short time, maybe, but in the end, it was like it had happened overnight – she showed up one day at the door, and everyone was happy. Her father had turned his life over to Christ and her mother seemed to gloat silently that she was right – one day he would learn. She only figured out later that it was Helena's difficulties that threw them in a frenzy of "what had gone wrong?", "what had they done to deserve this?" Her mother insisted on the idea that God was punishing her, while her father kept searching for some kind of logical explanation that justified their daughter's troubles.

The fear was hard to shake. But Tom was no threat. He was her only hope at this time of her life, but she didn't expect what was to happen next over dinner. When he spoke, she found herself clamoring for words on how to respond so she would seem smart, good, even witty. Tom broke a moment of silence with a cough. He stared at her as she took a bite of salad, then spoke.

"So have you talked to Elise?"

"No. She hasn't returned any of my calls. Not that I really want to hear from her. I know why she's avoiding me."

"So she hasn't given anything up to you?"

"No. Why would she?"

"Well…" Tom couldn't help but smirk. "You want to make her suffer?"

Helena couldn't help but laugh.

"How do you mean?"

"I would do anything to get rid of her."

"Okay, no way, I'm not getting involved."

"Why not?"

"What did you have in mind?"

At that point, Helena couldn't help but be drawn in. He was pretty clever, this Tom Overton, not just another pretty face. He leaned in and as the evening drew to a close, Helena found herself resolved to play in Tom's game, cementing him in his role as her partner in crime. And so the tables would be turned, and Elise would pay her dues.

"It doesn't have to be that serious," said Helena.

"Okay, think about it. Sleep on it, and tell me what you're thinking tomorrow."

Helena finished her crème brulee, and took a trip to the Ladies. Upon returning, she arrived at the table to find a receipt on her side of the table. Curious, she picked it up and stared. It was her part of the tab, her meal, drink and dessert neatly typed and added up to a total plus tax. She looked up at Tom who was looking away, almost purposely or ashamedly? He then wiped his mouth with a napkin and got up to go to the rest-room without a word to her. She sat and pulled her debit card from her wallet and set it on the receipt. The waitress came by about a minute later and swooped up the bill, with a curt smile and thank you. Tom remained absent. She was in disbelief which soon turned into complacence. She signed her receipt and looked up to see Tom returning to the table. She smiled nervously and he smiled back.

"Ready?" He asked.

"Yeah."

As they stepped outside, Tom made his way quickly to the car. Helena climbed in. The ride home was littered with small talk and awkward moments of silence. When they pulled into her driveway. Tom then leaned in and kissed her.

A few days later, Helena called Tom.

"About Elise, I don't want to do it," she said.

"Yeah, okay. It's your call." he said.

∾

Elise sat at her desk, trying to remember her password to get into the New York Post so she could read Page Six. She had dreams of moving there, a nice little apartment in Manhattan, where she could pursue her dream of becoming editor at a top notch publication. Reading the local papers from there made her feel like she was "in the know," and all she needed to do was, get a job, pack up, and move. From there, everything else would fall into place. She had the knowledge, the know how, and the street cred, now all she needed was a clean break from where she was now. Yeah, it was time to leave the Golden State, and get a bite of the Big Apple. How exciting! Just thinking of it uplifted her spirits.

So while a change of scenery might make her look good, it might not help as much in dealing with what was going on inside. And she knew the feeling as it crept up on her: guilt – for what she had done to her best friend. So-called best friend? Or simply, Helena Park? Tom had breezed in and out of the newsroom all week, as they ignored each other, as usual, she felt a tinge of sadness and heartache. She noticed however that Tom was in good spirits, more so than before, when he had first started. She didn't like that. When anyone got too happy, it was cause for suspicion. No one can be *that* happy.

She hadn't heard from Helena. Apparently she had given up on getting in touch with her. She found herself not caring that much. The apathy leaked over into her work. Others began to notice, but she pretended not to notice that they noticed. She made out like a drill sergeant, moving quickly, in a caffeine and Xanax filled subdued rage. Until one day, Shlabely called her into his office.

"You're fired."

He didn't want to explain, although he secretly knew that she was pumped full of drugs, whether they were prescribed or not, it was painfully obvious to everybody. Tom smirked, it was seren-dipity, pure and simple.

∾

"No need for the sabotage of Elise after all," Tom said smugly to Helena.

"What happened?"

"She got fired."

Helena sat up and looked at him.

"Are you serious?"

"Yeah."

Helena blinked, and scooted her back toward the headboard. She leaned and brought her knees up to her chest.

"I wonder what she's going to do?" she mused.

"Who cares…"

Tom straddled her and was laughing. His eyes crinkled at the corners and Helena, for the first time, began to see how kind of arrogant Tom was, borderline cocky. She winced and pushed him off. She got dressed and went into the kitchen and sat at the table.

"Something wrong?"

She paused for a moment.

"No."

He disappeared into his room and returned holding a cigarette. He lit it with a lighter and inhaled.

"Where'd you get that?"

"I had it, in my wallet. You want some?" he held out the joint to her. She smelled the musky scent of the drug fill the kitchen.

'No, thanks."

He shrugged and leaned against the wall, puffing away. He got up and looked in the refrigerator. She stared at him as he surveyed the contents and looked him up and down. She squinted her eyes and studied him.

"When was the last time you went shopping?"

She didn't answer. He sat at the table across from her. They stared at each other.

"What made you want to write?" Helena asked.

Tom raised his eyebrows, wondering where such a question came from, so suddenly.

"Um, not sure. I think it was my disillusionment with being a young urban professional for so many years."

"Really."

"Yeah. I just kind of wanted to break away, you know, like go live as a monk in Tibet or something."

"Hm."

His grandly philosophical notions came off as a bit cliché to Helena, who, at one time, had wanted to "break away" as well. It happens to everyone at some time in their lives.

"Speaking of Tibet, we should go away together sometime soon."

"Oh, yeah? What did you have in mind?"

"How about Korea?"

Helena was slightly surprised.

"Yeah, maybe."

"Ever been?"

"Yeah, when I was little, but I can't really remember," she said. She was tired and weary. It was then that her neurosis began. What was she doing with him? What had she seen in him? They had been together for only two months now, but his electric charm was not really charm but false pretense. His eyes were more cold than deep. No, he was nice! A decent bloke who was easy to talk to! He was interested in her "background."

"You really want to go to Korea?" she asked.

"Sure."

"OK, maybe."

17

~

As soon as the fall leaves began to fall, Christmas lights went up and the last season marker a la ritual before the start of a new year began. Christmas crept up this year, as Helena made her way through the behemoth known as The Mall, aka, the nightmare before Christmas. She navigated through the crowds: rich housewives peering over their lenses at the diamond studded Cartier watches in glass cases, appearing both serious and stand-offish, young twenty-something girls in tight jeans and clutching Coach bags, revealing belly necklaces and bare midriffs, at the only place where it was 75 degrees outside even in winter. The wave of perfume and the harsh bright lighting began to give Helena a headache, when she spotted, as she was waiting in line to make a purchase, the back of a woman's head who looked all too familiar.

"Elise?"

The woman turned around and caught Helena's eye.

"Helena, hi."

She was worn down and haggard. Helena couldn't believe she had let herself go like that. Her eyes were puffy and she looked worried. She appeared to have gained some weight. She didn't know that Helena knew about she and Tom, and she also didn't know she was now with him. They stared at each other, speechless.

"Well, it's...been a while," started Helena.

"Yeah, I know. Sorry." It was meant to apply to Helena for what she had done. Helena got it, but ignored it.

"Oh, well." She answered.

"How have you been?" asked Elise.

"Pretty good. Yourself?"

"Alright," a woman shoved her way in between them and nearly knocked Elise over.

She emerged and felt the need to escape, quickly.

"I'm sorry, I've got to go."

"Okay. Bye."

Helena watched her turn around and studied her retreating figure as it got smaller and eventually became lost in the crowd.

Helena sighed. She felt a sudden urge to cry, but held back. The truth was: she missed her.

⚘

Plunk. Tom threw down a pile of brochures onto Helena's lap.

"A History of Korea," "Traveling Seoul-O" Lonely Planet's, "Guide to Korea."

"And your point is?" Helena said.

"Why don't you want to go?" Tom asked.

"I dunno. I travel so much at work, I'm tired, that's all."

"Don't you have relatives over there that you want to see?"

"Yeah…"

"What, you don't want me to meet them?"

"They'll wonder why I'm not married yet."

"Do you care?"

"No, not really."

Tom laughed.

"What do you mean?"

"They expect you to have a family, and a $50,000 plus salary by the time your 25."

"Well you've got them on one count.'

"No, I'm ten years too late. It's unheard of for a 35-year-old woman to be single."

"Are they that behind the times?"

"Actually, no. I read somewhere that these days a lot of Korean women are ditching marriage for their careers, so the men have been flocking to Vietnam and Singapore for wives."

"Really?"

"Yeah, I think they're finally getting a clue."

Tom could not help it. He realized he was in love with her.

He sat in a chair across from her and motioned with his hand to come to him. She paused, and stared in his eyes. Eventually, she stood up and hovered over him. He took her hand and sat her down in his lap. He reached up with both hands and cupped her face.

"Will you marry me?"

Helena froze. It had been six months. She lowered her head into his so that their foreheads were touching. A meeting of the minds, it was not, but she feigned sincerity. She began nodding, and as soon as she saw confidence in Tom's eyes, she said, smiling:

"No."

Tom immediately pushed her off and stood up.

"What is wrong with you? You made me love you, and now you reject me?" he fumed.

"Okay," Helena raised her hand. "Enough."

"I thought you were in love with me. You were hinting toward it, I felt it."

"I can't explain it."

She got up to leave. She pulled her scarf around her neck, and before leaving said:

"I wasn't *hinting* about anything. You obviously read me wrong."

Tom picked up a brochure and threw it at her.

"I'm sorry," she said, and she meant it.

෴

It had been four weeks, five days, and three hours, since the fight had ensued with Helena. Tom was curled up in bed, blinds drawn, unshaven and lying in his underwear. Old pizza boxes littered his kitchen, and he dragged himself out of bed to make coffee.

He checked his answering machine, Helena had still not called. He had had plenty of time to assess the situation, and was sick with confusion and heartache. He was tired of figuring women out, wondering why things had gone wrong with Helena. He thought he had done everything right. She had wanted him. Was he expecting too much by asking her to marry him? He was lonely. He thought of Lucy. Too bad he had thrown away her number. She was a thousand miles away anyway. He stood up from the table, and decided he had let this go on long enough. He threw away the trash that littered his room, opened the blinds, and headed for the bathroom to take a shower. He had officially finished his mourning. Screw Helena. The truth came to him as the hot stream of water hit his face: He didn't really care that much.

෴

Helena sat anxiously gripping her cell phone. About ten minutes had passed when the sound of her ringtone startled her. She looked at the caller ID. Rick?

"Hello?"

'Hi it's Rick."

"Oh. Hello."

"How are you?"

"Good. And you?"

"Good."

Helena paused, speechless.

"Well, was wondering if you want to have dinner on Saturday."

"Oh, yeah? Saturday? Sure, I could."

"Okay, pick you up and 7?"

"Yes, okay."

"I'll need directions."

"Oh, right. Um…4371 N. Palm. You can Google it."

"Alright, great. See you Saturday."

"Yeah, OK."

Had she just agreed to go on a date with Rick Lee? Sure, he was pleasant. Calm, unassuming. Borderline boring? She would soon find out. She took a deep breath and swore to prepare to investigate. Rick Lee, Rick Lee. Who was Rick Lee? She wondered why Tom had not returned her call. He must hate her. She felt her stomach churn, and wondered if she was making a big mistake. He was her destiny, wasn't he?

∾

The restaurant was classy. It felt like old school 1920s, the time of prohibition and underground mob joints. Helena felt an air of coldness from Rick, a kind of stand-offishness masquerading as politeness. He was kind enough, and if he was nervous, he did not show it at all. He was quite calm, cool and collected as they say, and stared at her from across the table with a knowing smile. Helena gave a curt half-smile back to him, and suddenly felt scared. He had a quiet kind of authoritarian way about him, Helena noticed. In a way, she interpreted as something like, "he could do no wrong." But on the upside, he was just underneath Grant in rank, and had earned his keep fair and square for the past 10 years at Advent.

"So," he began the conversation, "will you be having a drink?"

"No, thank you," Helena replied.

"You don't drink?"

"No, I don't."

"Hm." He judged her momentarily. Then he ordered a shot of Remy Martin and a beer for himself. Helena looked away, then down, and rubbed the back of her neck nervously.

"Do you come to this restaurant often?" she asked.

"No, every once in a while."

The waitress came around and took their orders. They waited patiently, crunching on a fried calamari appetizer.

"You look beautiful tonight. I like your dress," remarked Rick.

Helena became nervous.

"Thank you."

She stared at him as he looked around the restaurant while sipping his beer.

"It's funny that we have worked in the same place for so long and have never really known each other," said Rick.

"Yes, it's easy to get absorbed in your work and let others just pass you by."

"What do you like about it?"

"Well, I like helping other companies get on their feet, increase their bottom line, flourish. It's almost like having a baby and watching it grow."

"Interesting analogy. But makes sense."

Helena felt a pull toward Rick, but she resisted. When their entrees arrived, she ate quickly, but realized that she didn't have much of an appetite.

She felt a sudden urge to flee. Out of the chair, out through the doors of the restaurant, on her way home. What was she doing? She stared at Rick and felt slightly repulsed, she didn't know why. Images of Tom surfaced in her memory.

When they had finished the meal, mostly in silence, Rick took the check immediately and paid.

As they made their way to the car, Rick put his arm around her. When they arrived at the passenger side door, he kissed her gently and opened the door for her and held her hand as if she were a princess getting into a carriage. She sat and waited for him to get in on his side of the car, and when he did, she reached over and held his hand as they pulled out. Thoughts of Tom swam into her psyche, and she tried to stamp them out. She glanced at Rick quickly and felt a warmth that tingled through her hand up into her arm and into her heart. It wasn't love, it was distraction, she decided. The pull she had felt earlier was justified. She was on the rebound.

∾

Dawn broke and morning came quickly. Helena had slept so soundly her awakening seemed to come too soon.

"Coffee?"

Rick was already up and had taken a shower. He set a freshly brewed cup of coffee on the bed-side table.

"I'm sorry but I've got to go."

"What? So soon?"

"Yeah, golf game, in Irvine."

"Oh, really? OK." She sat up and took a sip of coffee. He kissed her on the forehead and left. She stared at his retreating back as it nearly fled her bedroom like a friendly ghost.

And so the pattern repeated itself for the next three months. The sex was great, but the end-ing was always the same: Rick fleeing from her bedroom like a criminal in flight from the police. She didn't think anything of it. He was business-like, polite, swift and neat. Except when he drank, he became slightly sloppy, temperamental, maudlin. One night, he crashed on top of her, moaning, "Why? Helena? Why?" She shook him and asked, "Why what?" To which he replied, unceremoniously: "Nothing." Helena speculated to herself. Why her? Why him? Why tonight? Why any night? It was easy to ask why, but if you never answered the why question, you would never get anywhere – until that last Friday, when she was at Rick's house in Redondo Beach. Helena was up and had just taken a shower, when upon exiting the bathroom ran right smack into Rick, who shoved her into the tub and closed the curtains.

"What are you doing?"

"SHHHH..Just stay where you are!" He left. Helena heard voices in the bedroom. A woman with was berating Rick in an English accent.

"WHERE IS SHE? WHAT ARE YOU DOING? GET HER OUT OF HERE!"

Footsteps came trumping toward the bathroom to which Helena responded by crouching as low as she could into the corner of the tub, clutching her towel. The bathroom door flew open and in came the woman, like a raging bull, and threw open the shower curtains. Helena closed her eyes and waited to be pummeled.

"THERE SHE IS! GET OUT OF THERE! HOW DARE YOU!"

The woman had long curly blond hair and was wearing a beige business suit. She had horn-rimmed glasses and a red pout for a mouth.

"GET OUT!" She screamed, and grabbed Helena by the hair.

"OUCH, get off me! Who are you? Rick, who is she?"

"I'm his fiancée!'

"WHAT?' She turned to Rick and punched him squarely in the nose.

"Ah," he whimpered. "I'm sorry, Helena! I'm so sorry."

Helena stood there, threw off her towel and marched naked into the bedroom to find her clothes. The woman tended to Rick, and then shooed Helena away, with more insults.

Helena exited the house, fuming. She realized that she got the answer to Rick's eternal question "Why?"

As she started her car, the woman came flying out of the house, with something in her hand. Holy mother of God, it was a gun. Helena backed out quickly and screeched out of the driveway. The woman was pointing it at her and chasing the car down. Helena peeled out and escaped the once happy suburb, and as she reached the freeway, began to shake in terror.

"It's okay, it's okay," she kept telling herself, when really what she wanted to do was run her car off a cliff. She screamed.

"Rick you SON OF A BITCH!"

∽

The next evening, Helena was taking a bath, trying to recuperate from the trauma endured from the day before at Rick's house. Engaged! She couldn't believe it. These days you need a bullshit detector before you even greet someone hello.

Tom peered over a rosebush and loosened a thorn from his glove. Where was she? He had seen her disappear into the hallway and so she was either in her bedroom, or the bathroom. He scrambled his way to find another window, but realized his best port of entry was the open French windows that shot a clear view to the living room where she watched television. He waited. Ever since he had found out that Helena was romancing another guy, he became obsessed and began calling and visiting her home.

"YOU belong to ME!" Tom seethed, holding her by the shoulders.

"Get out Tom! Stop calling me! Stop coming over!" Helena had shot back.

Tom felt driven by a dozen demons called jealousy, obsession, anger, fear, loneliness, heartbreak, anxiety, lust, doom, self-destruction. Sure, he had the freedom of choice, but when he realized that who he really wanted was Helena, he broke down. He felt a pull toward her like a lion to its prey, and all he kept thinking about was her tenderness, her delicacy, her warmth. He just *wanted* it, dammit! How could anyone else have the privilege of having her? He was the only one for her.

"I really don't think we're right for each other," she had explained one day over coffee at a nearby café. It was a cloudy day, overcast, the kind of overcast that hurt your eyes by it's subdued light, but was too dark to wear sunglasses.

"What do you mean?"

"You're…selfish, and trite. I thought I needed you, but…I don't."

"YOU wanted ME. I love you."

"No, you don't love me. You just want me."

"Same difference."

He reached over the table to hold her hand but she pulled away. She stood up.

"Sorry, it's over." As she walked away, Tom ran after her. He walked alongside her and bombarded her with questions.

"So who is this guy? How did you meet him? Is it serious?"

She ignored him. She stopped by a liquor store and bought a pack of cigarettes. She stared ahead as she lit one, and resumed walking, Tom still in tow.

"I just want to know if you're going to marry him. Because I'm telling you right now, that no one could treat you better than I could. If you're with me, you'll be free, you will get anything you want, you will thrive and succeed."

Helena kept walking, staring straight ahead. She faltered for a moment and wiped a tear from her face. In the months that she and Tom were together she had never felt so ambivalent. She was ecstatic to be with him, but soon the novelty of his presence wore thin, like an old designer chair that you love to look at but is uncomfortable when you actually sit on it.

In bed at night, she would stare at him. His face took on an angelic quality, but she noticed the stubble, an acne scar, gray hair. Still handsome, but day after day he began to fill out, and pop out to her, like a 3-D movie. His apartment was filled with expensive furniture most of which he said he got as a "deal" from a friend back home, a furniture sales manager who paid in furniture what Tom sold him in marijuana. Tom had a stash so large, Helena worried he would get raided by the police sooner or later.

"Do you pay for anything?" she had asked once.

"Yeah, of course I do. That's kind of a stupid question."

"No. I mean, everyday living expenses, sure, but you have so many...customers."

"No, it just happens that way, by chance. It's America, baby."

At that point, Tom lit a joint and held it out to Helena She waved no and lay across his bed staring at the ceiling. She turned and looked at the large American flag hung up on the wall. Her gaze dropped to Tom's golden hair and finely built torso. She wanted to marry him, right then and there. He put on some music and began to dance. He had three tennis balls and began to juggle. She watched. She began laughing and he stopped. He laid on top of her and began kissing her. They stripped off their clothes and made love, purposefully and passionately.

Three months in and he started with the mumbo jumbo about visiting Korea and marriage. He had this plan about sabotaging Elise, and wanted to run off together. Helena, as upset as she was about Elise's dishonesty and betrayal, had no real desire to participate in a scheme to end her livelihood. Tom had insisted but to Helena's relief, the plan had been scrapped when Tom told her she had been fired on her own accord. His eagerness to hurt and humiliate someone could be justified, in this case, but she saw how his enthusiasm to hurt her was more evident than to teach her a lesson. That's when she started to question his morality.

Two weeks after Helena saw Elise in the department store, she got a collect call from her at 1 in the morning.

"Hi, it's Elise."

"Where are you, what's going on?"

"I need help Helena."

"With what?"

"Money. Can you wire me about a hundred dollars? I'll pay you back."

"Shit, Elise. No, no I can't. Sorry."

Helena hung up the phone. Five minutes later, it rang again.

"Hello?"

"Helena, It's Elise again. Listen. I know you know about Tom and me. I'm really sorry. You're the best friend I've ever had –"

"Not anymore."

"Just wire me the money Helena! I'll pay you back!"

"Why don't you ask Tom?"

"Screw you!"

"Screw ME?"

"I need help, Helena, please, have a heart."

"OK, I'll go pick you up and we can discuss this like two normal human beings. Where are you?" Helena got up and pulled on a pair of jeans.

"New York."

Helena's jaw dropped.

"Good luck." She hung up.

She kept mum about the Elise situation to Tom. She wondered why Elise was so down on her luck. It worried her slightly, but she meant it when she said they weren't exactly best friends anymore.

Tom had waited for Helena to look his way and answer his questions. She made her way through the parking lot and to her car, and Tom finally stopped following her. Her silence only made him more wanton and lustful, but in a vengeful angry way, not a fiery passionate way. In other words, she made him feel completely crazy and abnormal. He both hated and loved her. That is where his obsession began.

Helena wasn't quite sure why she had ended things with Tom. Remembering the situation with Rick, she sat in the bathtub, feeling incredibly down on her luck. There were times when she felt halfway crazy. She was on her way, again. As much as she tried to hold it in, she wept, her tears rolling down her face and into the bathwater. It was like a torrent and she covered her face with her hands as her body shook. She wanted to get out of town for a while, take some vacation time and just leave everything. She stopped crying and realized that was exactly what she needed. She leaned forward and pulled out the tub stopper to drain the tub. She would have a private conference with Grant on Monday, and hopefully, get her down time.

Tom was still outside, and pulled up his pants. He had just urinated in the rose bushes and felt a tad guilty, but didn't have a choice. He peered into the window and watched Helena walk into the living room in her pajamas. She sat on the couch and turned on the TV. He watched her intently, wondering how he could strategize in getting her back. An hour later, his lids grew heavy and he began to nod off. It was another uneventful night of spying and wishful thinking. As he made his way out of the foliage, he began to get angry at himself for not coming up with some kind of plan. He was satisfied enough by just staring at her from afar. It was safe, and he was turned on by the notion of being a sort of outlaw. Had he risen to the level where he could actually call himself a "peeping tom?" Was he ill?

He made his way out of the bushes and walked a half a block down the road to his car. He certainly felt like a criminal in his black cap and clothing. He had already confronted her, she was clearly over him. But how? So quickly. As he drove home, he felt his whole world crashing down on him, and he began to feel slow, lethargic, depressed. When he arrived home, he fell into bed. He actually cried.

18

~

Helena was free. She was driving north in her silver Saab convertible. The blue sky was cloudless, and she found herself wanting to stare up at the expansive sky, and not the road ahead of her. Northern California always welcomed her, with the cool weather, familiar freeways and the romantic nostalgia that passed through her when crossing the bay bridge into San Francisco.

Grant didn't give her too much heat for asking for the week off. It was vacation time well-earned, but more than that, she had to figure something out, for herself.

The phone conversation was stupid, but short and sweet. She tracked him down through the Internet, and he actually was at the same number he had been at for years. There was a tinge of surprise and, she might even venture to call "delight" when he found out it was her. But he still had his way of acting very cool whenever she was around.

She had booked a hotel room in a central area of the city, not wanting to risk having him invite her to spend the night at his place. No, a hotel room was the necessary back-up plan, especially when visiting someone like Shawn.

It had been about five years since she had seen him, running into him once on the street, which was a rare feat in itself, but she took no pretense in believing it was fate or a sign from God. They caught each other's eye at the stop walk. Techies with bluetooths and Chinese grandmas bustled in between them and they stared at each other from their respective side of the street, knowing something but remaining calm, both probably trying to mask their innate sense of fear. Whether he felt the fear or not was debatable, but that was what Shawn made Helena feel: Fear. When the light changed, they walked past each other, and he looked into her eyes, just as she looked up, and Helena lingered her gaze long enough to see him smirk. She wondered whether he was secretly laughing, or whether it was some kind of authoritarian message of approval.

The fact that they had passed each other on the street without so much as a nod, or a hello was a sign in itself, that neither of them really cared that much about each other. The fact that he had not grabbed her arm and stopped her and that she had not done so either, reinforced that idea. The fact that they passed each other on a crosswalk was the perfect excuse, because had they stopped and done so, the rhythm would have been interrupted, the symphony broken, the steady beat of the accepted lunacy of city life, people running away and back to each other, kissing and kicking – it was a metaphor for the insanity that comes with some kind of dysfunctional romance. So indeed it was a sign, and it showed that Helena was far from her belief that she was solidly grounded in reality. It was that sort of magical thinking that got her into trouble. It was not meant to be.

Or was it?

❧

He was standing outside the restaurant, hands in his pockets, leaning against a wall. He was wearing khakis, a v-neck sweater over a t-shirt, and converse high tops. He was edging towards 42 and still dressed like a teenager. He turned his head and caught her eye. He neither smiled nor did he seem at all happy to see her. He simply stared at her with a look that seemed to say: "Yeah, so, what do you have for me now?"

As she came closer toward him, he strode toward her, and they stopped about a foot away from each other, like two soldiers ready to salute. She blinked.

"Hi," she ventured.

"Hey."

About 30 seconds passed before she said:

"Well, do you want to go inside?"

"Sure."

They stepped inside the restaurant and got a table. They sat and stared at each other, before he finally piped up:

"They have a good lemon coconut milk soup here."

"OK."

She looked at her menu.

"Tom Kum Kai."

God, had she been this bored when she was with him? The conversation seemed to hit a dead end each time she ventured forth. His eyes took on a stoned glazed quality. After another ten minutes of silence, she found herself itching to leave as soon as possible. She looked at him and squinted. He had seemed so small, leaning up against the wall, and then as he walked toward her, he looked up at her as if he were upset, or angry.

They ate in virtual silence, and when the tab arrived, she paid for her half with cash.

They ventured outside and stood awkwardly, watching the cars drive by. The city began to light up as the day grew into night.

"You wanna get a beer?"

She hesitated before saying:

"Nah."

"We can go to my place and get high."

Helena had not yet told him that she had sworn off all drugs, no matter how "relaxed" it might make her, or rather, "defenseless." But something inside her stirred, she wanted to grasp on to something intangible, not answers necessarily, but a feeling.

"OK."

They walked down the street together toward his house, buried somewhere in the cozy neighborhoods that were entwined through the miniature city landscape of a bustling college town. The silence had grown comfortable, and she ventured to break it.

"Have you moved much?" she asked.

"Once, since grad school."

"Do you have roommates?"

"No."

They continued to walk, as he pulled her into a neighborhood, around the corner, and the sounds of car engines and the chatter of drunken college students exiting restaurants and breweries faded fast against the softer sounds of trees rustling in the night breeze and the slapping of their shoes against the concrete. Lights lit up in the houses exposed that hidden home life of people she did not know, televisions lit up and flashing in the windows. They finally arrived, at a run down two-story house that could pass for Victorian, but was much too rickety to even deserve such a distinguished label. He jiggled the keys in the lock, and the door creaked open. He entered first and held the door open, as she walked in. His room was on the right, and he walked in, turning on a light. There was a futon mattress on the floor, a couch, and not much else.

He foraged into a drawer and pulled out rolling papers, and a bag of marijuana. He rolled a cigarette and lit it. He passed it on to her, and she took it, and held it between her fingers. She stared at it and gave it back.

"I can't really have any."

"Why not?"

"Doctor's orders."

"You sick?"

"Yeah. You could say that."

He didn't probe the subject further, and continued to drag on the joint.

They sat down on the couch next to each other. She stared straight ahead but felt his head turn toward her, staring at her profile. She knew the moment she turned, what would happen, and so she didn't. But he leaned in anyway, and she felt his breath on her cheek, the smell of the cigarette wafting past her nostrils. Just an inch more in and he kissed her cheek. He stubbed out the joint in an ashtray and then went in for the kill, a soft peck on the lips and then his hand on her thigh. Reaching toward the buttons on her pants, he opened them and began to unzip. She stopped him abruptly and pulled away. She still did not dare to look at him. He stopped as if in slow motion, and relit the joint. He sat back, carelessly, staring up at the ceiling and inhaling. She buttoned her pants and stared around at his room. It had the same bohemian quality she remembered - comfortably messy.

"Is there a reason why you called me?" he asked.

"I just wanted to know how you were doing."

He tried to kiss her again. She stood up and walked toward the door.

"I don't know why. You never really had much to say."

"What do you mean?"

"I mean, we sort of disintegrated, you know. I don't even know what we were really about."

"Well, maybe you should come over here and I'll show you." He patted the couch and began to laugh. It was a cheesy line, and then she realized what the attraction was. That sort of sordid power people can hold over each other when they fall into these sort of ridiculous roles, like she, the impressionable teenager, and he, the lonely rebel hermit, who denied everything sweet and kind, and fed the fire of bitterness and cruelty disguised as rebellion. It was kind of a turn on, surrendering to the drama, giving way to wanton scenarios and fantastical images that would one day be remembered with lust, or malice, or both.

She sauntered around his room. He remained glued to the couch, watching her every move, like a vulture or a hawk. Vultures fed on the remains of the dead, he had possibly found delight in killing her long ago. But she remained steadfast and strong, determined to make sense of this cloudy part of her past, one she remembers only in bits and pieces, like a puzzle of parties, drugs, kisses, sex, sex and more sex. She did not want to make a profound discovery, with a moment of clarity and a smile with her face toward the sunset. She simply wanted to feel resolved without giving in to her resentment, one that would later start a fight, make her feel vicious and vengeful. She was past that, wasn't she? And so, she turned to him and asked:

"Why did you leave that one day, when I was crying – "

"You were always crying," he interjected.

She paused.

"No, no I wasn't."

"I don't remember what you're talking about." He paused and stared at her with a serious gaze.

"Then why –"

"I don't know."

He waited for her to reply. When she didn't, he stood up and sauntered out of the room. She heard the clunking of pots and pans. He was cooking something.

She stayed in the bedroom, and began opening drawers, looking for something that would give her a clue as to why he was the way he was. She found nothing. She eyed the closet and made her way toward it. It seemed to glow, like the forbidden entry to the treasure. It loomed before her as she inched closer and closer. She placed her hand on old creaky doorknob, and opened it. Inside, she found his clothes, hanging placidly. She glanced around, and found a stack of magazines about a foot high. She dug deeper. Just underneath his Bad Religion and Clash t-shirts was a gun. Helena's stomach churned and she thought she might become very ill. She wanted to throw up. She heard footsteps and quickly jumped out of the closet and closed the door behind her.

"Hello. Are you cooking?"

"Yeah. I've got some lentil soup on the stove."

She ventured closer to him as he made his way out the door. She followed him.

"So, how's life in social work?" She was studying his every movement without his knowledge, staring at him up and down, judging, wondering, scrutinizing.

"OK."

"Mm hmm. You still into that animal rights thing? Still a vegetarian?"

"Yup."

"Yeah, cruelty toward animals is a shame. You could even argue that cruelty toward humans is even more of a crime, but people always find a way to justify such misdemeanors, whereas animals cannot, and have no defense. Take for example, hunting, where we SHOOT animals with GUNS for sport." She paused staring at him and waiting for a flinch, she noticed he froze slightly.

"I think the soup is ready."

"None for me, thanks."

"It's interesting," she continued. "The compassion that people claim to have for all sentient beings can be overridden by anger and insensitivity."

"What do you mean?"

"Well, how do you assess your life as someone in the helping profession, when you, are absolutely and totally devoid of feeling for others, for example, me, circa 1995?"

"I haven't thought about it much."

"You never thought much about anything. You have like a zero hindsight for everything you do."

She went on.

"I believed you when you said that you loved me –"

"I never said that."

"In a round about way, you did. You kept me around, but you never gave, you just took."

"What was it you wanted?"

"Commitment."

He was silent for a moment.

"You never considered where I was coming from," she continued. "You just wanted what you wanted the way you wanted it. You didn't even want to be known as my boyfriend."

Helena remembered how it was. It was trickery, the work of a con artist, lies, hypocrisy, and a cover up. The trail led to his door, but he justified himself by saying it was more or less her fault for feeling the way she did. It was like trying to hit a moving target. Nothing made sense after a while, and then the situation would just disappear like it never happened in the first place.

Her thoughts went to what she had found in the closet. He was definitely crazy, out of whack, a paradox. She watched as he poured his soup into a bowl, and as he sat down to eat it, she stood up and announced:

"I better be going." It was a test.

"Why?"

"I feel like if I stay, I'll never want to leave. The truth is, Shawn, I still love you." Still testing. She waited anxiously.

He sat there, stunned.

"I miss you." She said. Was he going to pass?

As soon as she said it, he sat stone faced, like a miserable statue. He looked down, momentarily, then looked up at her and said,

"I love you too."

So it was real. He had matured. She could sense words coming out of his mouth, but he was still afraid to let them out. She knew why. Flashes of scenery shuttered through her mind like a film noir art flick. Was there ever a moment when she was kind of, dare she say, happy? Sure, many moments, but she still felt a wall in her mind, where she did not dare go, but the only thing she could do, was forget. When she thought about life like a series of images, headphones on and scenes melting with music, she felt better. It kept her from reality, but she could not escape this.

Helena felt a tug in her heart. She stared at him and asked:

"Do you care if I stay or go?"

"No."

She went back to his room and picked up her bag. She entered the kitchen and stared solemnly into his face.

"I'll be going then," she said, blinking uneasily. He stared at her, his eyes like those on a dead fish.

She turned her back to him and headed toward the door. She was leaving, the last and final time. She left his cold room, his shoddy furnishings, his rickety house. With that last step down the stairs, she finally knew. She fled, and never looked back.

∾

The ride home was sobering. Helena felt herself reemerging from some kind of cocoon, or shedding skin, ready for a new phase of life. She had left the city early and the sun was just peeking through the clouds. The sky looked extraordinarily blue that day, and she marveled at the expansiveness of it, reaching from city to city, country to country, it was one thing that would remain constant in life, wherever she went, she could always count on a blue sky. It reminded her of when she visited New York with two friends from college. They had split up, each wanting to follow their own agenda. As she wandered the busy New York City streets, she had ended up at the Empire State Building. She only glanced upward, marveling at the height and strength of that building. It was odd, she realized, that she was absolutely alone, not a soul was seen wandering around. And so, she stared up at the building. She sucked in her breath, and almost lost it. The building seemed to sway from side to side, reaching up into that expansive blue sky, and loomed above her. She caught her breath, and found herself unable to take her eyes off of it, or to sit up. She stood there for nearly half an hour, unable to tear herself away. She marveled at such height, such strength, such beauty. If she could be so strong and tall had yet to be seen. She stared into the blue sky and, head in the clouds, she hoped one day she would grow into success, wonder, magnificence, something that she could be proud of.

She cruised down the long highway, staring straight ahead, while the road before her stretched on and carried her home.

∾

When she returned to her house, she found a pile of mail in the mailbox, and a long slim package on her doorstep. She carried her armload of mail into the house, fumbling to turn the doorknob from the garage into the house. She unloaded the pile of envelopes and magazines onto her kitchen table. She made her way to the front door, and opened it. The package lay there, like an ominous message from afar. It was wrapped in ribbon, in gold packaging. She picked it up and brought it inside. She opened it at once, eager to see its contents. A bouquet of wilted red roses lay inside, appearing sad and forlorn. She picked one up and stared at it, as the bud dropped its head downward. She rummaged through the package for a card - she needed some kind of explanation to relieve her of this tortured moment where the pounding in her chest made her mind think of love, or apologies. Which was it? She finally found it in a small square plain white envelope. She opened it, and read.

"So sorry. Please forgive me. I love you."

So it was both.

She almost avoided reading the from line, which blurred below her on the card like an anticipatory verdict. There was a *Love,* and then his name: *Rick.*

At that moment, she heard a knock on the door. Upon opening it, she found Rick, standing before her, a look of guilt and shame on his face.

"What do you want?" she asked, feeling some kind of valuable strength coursing through her, like an adage to her new found confidence, buoyed by her visit with Shawn.

"Did you –"

"Yeah, I got your flowers."

"Can I come in?" he asked, sheepishly. "I want to talk to you."

Helena pursed her lips and glared at him. She wondered if she should even give him a chance. That had never happened to her before. What made it worse was that they were co-workers, making an already sticky situation even stickier. She was glad to have had that week off to reconcile her feelings about Shawn, and was even more glad to have avoided seeing Rick at work, until now. There he was, standing there, eager to please, kind of like a scared puppy dog. Her thoughts ran through her head very fast, and what she realized she really wanted to do was slam the door in his face, but what she actually ended up doing was opening the door ajar so that he could make his way in. As he sauntered in, she turned to face the other way, then shut the door behind her. Rick turned to her and waited for her to walk before him, leading him where she wanted him to go. They entered the living room, and Helena perched herself on the couch, while Rick sat in a chair across from her.

"You see, the truth is, I have…issues," Rick confessed. "I don't really want to marry her. I thought she might be more manageable then the rest."

"Manageable?"

"No, I was engaged to this Korean woman, and I had never been with a Korean woman before. My parents are set on me marrying a Korean woman."

"I'm Korean."

"Yes, I know, but the more time I spent with her, the more miserable I became."

"Why?"

"She was the same as the rest. I went to Northwestern, and all those women I met and dated, they were snobbish, almost rude, and I fell for their act every time, just because they were both beautiful and smart. But the problem was, they didn't take me seriously. This girl, that one you met –"

"Was assaulted by," Helena corrected him.

"She was nice and sweet at first, but then she turned on me, and she started to get really aggressive and bossy about everything. I was hoping to God that she could be the one, but I slowly began to resent and hate her. I started doing things like going to strip bars and gambling. I gambled away half of our savings for the wedding, and after I did it, I felt bad, but then I felt relieved to have postponed the wedding which made her unhappy because I lowered our budget. After she found you and I, she called off the engagement."

He took out a cigarette from his shirt pocket, lit it and looked at her.

"I'm free now."

Helena stood up and walked over to him. She stroked his hair and hugged him, his head in her lap.

"What makes you think I will be any different? For the record, I'm pretty screwed up too."

"No, I know you understand, that's all. Those women I've been with, they don't seem to understand, or they didn't want to. You, you seem to have depth, you seem wise."

Helena took his hand and kissed it. They looked at each other and Helena saw how tired Rick looked. She noticed fine lines and wrinkles around his eyes. His eyes were sad, almost ghostly. Rick stood up to meet Helena face to face. He cupped her face and kissed her. They retreated to her bedroom and lay in bed together. In an entangled mass of limbs and hands, they disrobed and fell together, groping at each other for some kind of lost ideal.

∽

Helena opened her eyes and sat up in bed.

"Rick?"

The hallway light was on. Helena saw the flood of light come through the bedroom doorway. She got out of bed and put on her robe. She walked down the hallway, and into the kitchen. All the lights were off, and as she turned on the kitchen light, it illuminated the rest of the house, enough to see that Rick was nowhere to be found. Helena checked the clock on the wall and saw that it was 4 a.m. She sat at her kitchen table and stared into space. No note, nothing. Then she noticed something on the refrigerator. It was a note, hanging by a magnet, it said: "Helena, I can't stay tonight, will call you later."

She sighed and sat down. She poured herself a glass of water, and drained it. Then she went back to bed.

19

It was Monday. The alarm sounded at 7 a.m.
Helena dragged herself out of bed and began
to start her day. First, a shower, then coffee with
breakfast, while listening to the morning show on
TV. She felt renewed, her first day back to work
in a while, and she actually felt somewhat happy,
knowing that her time with Rick had not been in
vain. She started her car in the garage and backed
out slowly, rolling down her window, she breathed
in the fresh morning air and was on her way.

At the office, she saw Rick, who, had not called
like he had promised, obviously forgetting that
she would see him at work. Unless, he decided
to take the day off. She sauntered down the aisle,
past cubicles, and casually passed by his office.
He was there, on the phone, his chair swiveled to
face the window, so all she saw was the back of his
head. She smiled and made her way back to her
office. In those golden moments that passed as she
swiftly floated down the hallway, images flashed

before her, Tom, in bed, Tom, across from her in a restaurant, eating, Tom, laughing. Then her thoughts slowly began to transition to Rick, and she realized, she was over him. She felt all of a sudden, sick, thinking she had been in love, then a downward spiral, stunned by the reality of human beings, men, herself, reluctant and willing at the same time. Her head began to spin. She ran to the bathroom, scrambled toward a stall and vomited.

∞

And so it began, Helena had inadvertently created a sort of pattern for herself. Normally she would say screw self-help, who needs it, no, only 20 years ago, as a sprightly spontaneous teenager who felt she could do no wrong, and was invincible. But so it went, Helena had come to face her fears, to confront, to be rid of contempt prior to investigation, and to grow out of her leather and into silk. But it didn't mean that she had completely sold out, it simply meant that she would stop doing the same things and expecting different results, she had come up for water and was swimming with sharks. Soon, they would swim right past her, knowing she was one of them.

And so it goes, she returned home from work that day feeling heavy and tired. But she was determined to do the right thing, and come clean about what she had done to Tom. Apologize? She hated the very sound of the word, but she knew, deep inside, she had to. And anyway hadn't it turned out in her favor? Where Tom actually fell in love with her? And proposed marriage? And had she not run the opposite way, sabotaging the very plans she had created? That was what disturbed her the most – the repulsion of someone she thought so beloved, and how he deflated, like a sad blow-up doll, right in front of her eyes.

And so it goes, a month had passed, and some sort of security began to envelop her. But she knew she had to confront him sometime, if she was ever going to be completely at peace, and so, she picked up the phone and called him.

∾

Tom was packing his things, surrounded by boxes secured from U-Haul, the truck itself parked in an extra space near his apartment. They had thrown in some bubble wrap for good measure, but he didn't have very many valuables. Still, he put it to good use wrapping his kitchenware, glasses, ceramic plates and bowls. He looked around and wiped the sweat from his forehead, his third move in a year.

Tom had signed on to take some writing classes at a university in Los Angeles. He had never really had formal training, but then decided to bite the bullet and enroll. He was moving out of Sun Valley and into West L.A. His sentiment, was essentially, "screw everybody, I'm better than this" and was eager to put his skills to work in a bigger pond. He was here, so he may as well take advantage of it.

As he taped up a box, he heard his cell phone ring. He sprinted to the coffee table where he had placed it.

"Hello?"

"Hi Tom, it's Helena."

"Hi. What's going on?"

"I was wondering if you could meet for coffee sometime."

"Well, I'm kind of busy packing, but I could probably meet you, sure."

"OK, at that place near my house?"

"Sure."

"Saturday at 1?"

"OK."

Tom hung up and was caught off guard. He had thought she wanted nothing to do with him and he had sworn her off completely. He wondered why she wanted to see him.

∾

It had actually happened. She had not meant it to coincide with the appointment she had just made with Tom days earlier. But when the day came, and she had marked it in her date book, she had gotten much better at doing so because sometimes she forgot – her period, late. She bought a pregnancy test and – it had actually happened. She was pregnant.

She had reported the news to Rick just a day ago. As one might guess, he was stunned. It had only been a month, and they had seen each other a total of three times. As they sat together in her living room, Rick spent most of the time staring at the ground, in a state of disbelief. Then, of course, the big question:

"What are you going to do?"

Helena didn't miss it. She was well aware of the notion that she was alone, even if Rick claimed to be by her side. It was, "what are *you* going to do," and *not*, "what are *we* going to do."

Helena was still, admittedly, disappointed and she felt a sharp sting of anxiety, making her heart palpitate.

"I don't know yet."

She waited a beat, and knew he wasn't going to ask.

"I'm," he stuttered. "I can't, it's kind of a choice I've made. I'm sorry." He kissed her forehead and said, "But if there's anything you need, please let me know."

For some reason, Helena felt relief, but she felt it in her soul, she was sad. But did she really want that? Most women would, she guessed, but this would be on account of the baby, and not real love. And anyway, he had made a choice, not to marry.

He had had this resolve, apparently, for a while, but buckled under pressure from his parents to marry the woman that had found them that day. After that incident, he went right back to it, turning that parental pressure on its head. He didn't care anymore.

When he left, Helena was left with herself, wanting to respect Rick's choice, and halfway retreating from a proposal if one had been made. She really didn't know if she could raise the child herself, but the other options, to abort or give up for adoption were less appealing to her. She took a moment and found she couldn't hold back the tears, and wept quietly, before curling up on the couch, where she closed her eyes and silently prayed.

∾

Tom strode up to the café at exactly one minute past one, and Helena greeted him at an outside table.

"Hello!"

"Hi there, good to see you!"

They embraced, and Tom pulled out a chair and sat down.

"Well, you look good."

"Thank you."

"How have things been?"

"Good, busy."

"Mm hm."

The waiter came by to take their order. They stared at each other, and waited. Helena was surprised with Tom's serenity. He seemed to have matured. He looked at her and she could see some hurt in his eyes. She could feel the awkwardness of their reunion creeping up, and she forced herself to break the silence. She took off her sunglasses.

"Tom," she waited. He looked at her with bleary eyes, as if he were on the verge of tears. "I'm sorry."

He was silent.

"I know I apologized before for what happened, but I felt like I needed to let you know that despite what happened between us, I was at fault, too, for misleading you."

Tom hesitated and looked deep in thought.

"It wasn't just that, Helena, you ignored me, my deep seated feelings for you. You have this way of dismissing everyone and everything."

"I went after you, but I created something in the same way that I do business, and I applied it to you, like you were a prize. It was wrong."

"I think you have problems, Helena. I think you are a damaged person. You are."

Helena coughed and looked away. The drinks arrived, and Helena took a long sip. The caffeine would give her some fire, some spark that would let her get out of this conversation, still kicking.

"Have you been OK?" Tom asked.

Helena stared at the table, and then up at Tom. He was the same. He had that air of openness, kind eyes, a searching and genuine gaze. And so she trusted him. It was almost automatic, the way it came out.

"I'm pregnant."

Tom choked on his cappuccino.

"Are you serious?"

"Don't worry."

"Well, I'm not, it couldn't have been. It's been too long."

"Yes, I know."

And again – the question.

"What are you going to do?"

"I'm not sure." She had to make an effort to remain calm, when inside she was going crazy, sick with worry. But she dared not show it.

"Are you going to marry him?"

"No. He doesn't want to get married."

"Do you?"

She paused before answering. She felt the sun shining down on her, and she searched the blue sky, taking in the natural beauty that surrounded her.

"No, not really."

Tom searched her face. She seemed content and self-assured.

"I'm kind of afraid. I've never had to deal with kids much, I was an only child, and all our relatives with little kids, cousins, you know, they all lived out of town. We rarely saw them. I just don't know if I'm good with them."

"You could support one. You make enough money."

"True."

They remained silent and sipped their drinks.

"I think you should just have it."

Helena bit her lip and studied the ground.

"Maybe. But my parents…"

"What. They wouldn't approve?"

"No. I don't think they'd care."

"It's your life, you've been on your own forever. You're a successful middle-aged woman."

"Yeah, maybe you're right. Truthfully, I do want to keep it."

"It'll be the next great experiment in your life. Go for it. You'll be fine."

Helena felt reassured with a new found confidence. She let the sun shine into her eyes briefly. She looked out beyond the parking lot, the cars, the buildings and up into the cloudless sky.

Maybe she could start this next chapter of her life after all, she thought, smiling.

THE END